Acclaim for SUSAN MINOT's

LUST

& Other Stories

SUSAN MINOT

LUST

& Other Stories

Susan Minot is the author of
Monkeys, Folly, and *Evening.* She
lives in New York City.

LUST

Other Stories

· SUSAN MINOT ·

VINTAGE CONTEMPORARIES
Vintage Books
A Division of Random House, Inc.
New York

For Davis

FIRST VINTAGE CONTEMPORARIES EDITION, AUGUST 2000

Copyright © 1989 by Susan Minot

All rights reserved under International and Pan-American
Copyright Conventions. Published in the United States by Vintage
Books, a division of Random House, Inc., New York, and simultaneously
in Canada by Random House of Canada Limited, Toronto. Originally
published in the United States by Houghton Mifflin Company,
Boston, in 1989.

Published here by special arrangement with Houghton Mifflin Company.

Vintage is a registered trademark and Vintage Contemporaries and
colophon are trademarks of Random House, Inc.

Some of the stories in this book were originally published in the following
publications: *The Paris Review, Grand Street, New Generation,
Mademoiselle, Harper's Magazine,* and *Columbia Magazine.*

Library of Congress Cataloging-in-Publication Data
Minot, Susan.
Lust & other stories / Susan Minot.
p. cm.
Contents: Lust — Sparks — Blow — City night —
Lunch with Harry — The break-up — The swan in the garden —
The feather in the toque — The knot — A thrilling life — Ile sèche —
The man who would not go away.
ISBN 0-375-70925-8 (pbk.)
1. New York (N.Y.)—Social life and customs—Fiction.
2. Young adults—New York (State)—New York—Fiction.
I. Title: Lust and other stories. II. Title.
PS3563.I4755 L88 2000
813'.54—dc21   99-462087

Author photograph © Huger Foote

www.vintagebooks.com

Printed in the United States of America
10 9 8 7 6 5 4

Ah, I have asked too much, I plainly see.

OVID
The Loves

Acknowledgments

I would like, first of all, to thank Seymour Lawrence for being so kind as to publish me, Camille Hykes for being his assistant, and Fran Kiernan for seeing the manuscript through. Thanks also to my agent, Georges Borchardt, for his constant tranquility, and to Nancy Lemann for her loyal friendship, in literature and out. This book was written in various places on both sides of the Atlantic and many thanks go to those people who gave me rooms in which to write.

Finally, my most heartfelt thanks go to Ben Sonnenberg, whose advice, editorial and otherwise, is an integral part of this book.

Contents

■

■

■

ONE

Lust

LEO WAS FROM a long time ago, the first one I ever saw nude. In the spring before the Hellmans filled their pool, we'd go down there in the deep end, with baby oil, and like that. I met him the first month away at boarding school. He had a halo from the campus light behind him. I flipped.

Roger was fast. In his illegal car, we drove to the reservoir, the radio blaring, talking fast, fast, fast. He was always going for my zipper. He got kicked out sophomore year.

By the time the band got around to playing "Wild Horses," I had tasted Bruce's tongue. We were

3

clicking in the shadows on the other side of the amplifier, out of Mrs. Donovan's line of vision. It tasted like salt, with my neck bent back, because we had been dancing so hard before.

Tim's line: "I'd like to see you in a bathing suit." I knew it was his line when he said the exact same thing to Annie Hines.

You'd go on walks to get off campus. It was raining like hell, my sweater as sopped as a wet sheep. Tim pinned me to a tree, the woods light brown and dark brown, a white house half hidden with the lights already on. The water was as loud as a crowd hissing. He made certain comments about my forehead, about my cheeks.

We started off sitting at one end of the couch and then our feet were squished against the armrest and then he went over to turn off the TV and came back after he had taken off his shirt and then we slid onto the floor and he got up again to close the door, then came back to me, a body waiting on the rug.

You'd try to wipe off the table or to do the dishes and Willie would untuck your shirt and get his hands up under in front, standing behind you, making puffy noises in your ear.

*

4

He likes it when I wash my hair. He covers his face with it and if I start to say something, he goes, "Shush."

For a long time, I had Philip on the brain. The less they noticed you, the more you got them on the brain.

My parents had no idea. Parents never really know what's going on, especially when you're away at school most of the time. If she met them, my mother might say, "Oliver seems nice" or "I like that one" without much of an opinion. If she didn't like them, "He's a funny fellow, isn't he?" or "Johnny's perfectly nice but a drink of water." My father was too shy to talk to them at all unless they played sports and he'd ask them about that.

The sand was almost cold underneath because the sun was long gone. Eben piled a mound over my feet, patting around my ankles, the ghostly surf rumbling behind him in the dark. He was the first person I ever knew who died, later that summer, in a car crash. I thought about it for a long time.

"Come here," he says on the porch.

I go over to the hammock and he takes my wrist with two fingers.

"What?"

He kisses my palm then directs my hand to his fly.

Songs went with whichever boy it was. "Sugar Magnolia" was Tim, with the line "Rolling in the rushes / down by the riverside." With "Darkness Darkness," I'd picture Philip with his long hair. Hearing "Under My Thumb" there'd be the smell of Jamie's suede jacket.

We hid in the listening rooms during study hall. With a record cover over the door's window, the teacher on duty couldn't look in. I came out flushed and heady and back at the dorm was surprised how red my lips were in the mirror.

One weekend at Simon's brother's, we stayed inside all day with the shades down, in bed, then went out to Store 24 to get some ice cream. He stood at the magazine rack and read through *MAD* while I got butterscotch sauce, craving something sweet.

I could do some things well. Some things I was good at, like math or painting or even sports, but the second a boy put his arm around me, I forgot about wanting to do anything else, which felt like a relief at first until it became like sinking into a muck.

*

It was different for a girl.

When we were little, the brothers next door tied up our ankles. They held the door of the goat house and wouldn't let us out till we showed them our underpants. Then they'd forget about being after us and when we played whiffle ball, I'd be just as good as they were.

Then it got to be different. Just because you have on a short skirt, they yell from the cars, slowing down for a while, and if you don't look, they screech off and call you a bitch.

"What's the matter with me?" they say, point-blank.
  Or else, "Why won't you go out with me? I'm not asking you to get married," about to get mad.
  Or it'd be, trying to be reasonable, in a regular voice, "Listen, I just want to have a good time."
  So I'd go because I couldn't think of something to say back that wouldn't be obvious, and if you go out with them, you sort of have to do something.

I sat between Mack and Eddie in the front seat of the pickup. They were having a fight about something. I've a feeling about me.

Certain nights you'd feel a certain surrender, maybe if you'd had wine. The surrender would be forgetting yourself and you'd put your nose to his

7

neck and feel like a squirrel, safe, at rest, in a restful dream. But then you'd start to slip from that and the dark would come in and there'd be a cave. You make out the dim shape of the windows and feel yourself become a cave, filled absolutely with air, or with a sadness that wouldn't stop.

Teenage years. You know just what you're doing and don't see the things that start to get in the way.

Lots of boys, but never two at the same time. One was plenty to keep you in a state. You'd start to see a boy and something would rush over you like a fast storm cloud and you couldn't possibly think of anyone else. Boys took it differently. Their eyes perked up at any little number that walked by. You'd act like you weren't noticing.

The joke was that the school doctor gave out the pill like aspirin. He didn't ask you anything. I was fifteen. We had a picture of him in assembly, holding up an IUD shaped like a T. Most girls were on the pill, if anything, because they couldn't handle a diaphragm. I kept the dial in my top drawer like my mother and thought of her each time I tipped out the yellow tablets in the morning before chapel.

If they were too shy, I'd be more so. Andrew was nervous. We stayed up with his family album, sharing a pack of Old Golds. Before it got light, we turned on the TV. A man was explaining how to plant seedlings. His mouth jerked to the side in a tic. Andrew thought it was a riot and kept imitating him. I laughed to be polite. When we finally dozed off, he dared to put his arm around me, but that was it.

You wait till they come to you. With half fright, half swagger, they stand one step down. They dare to touch the button on your coat then lose their nerve and quickly drop their hand so you — you'd do anything for them. You touch their cheek.

The girls sit around in the common room and talk about boys, smoking their heads off.

"What are you complaining about?" says Jill to me when we talk about problems.

"Yeah," says Giddy. "You always have a boy-friend."

I look at them and think, As if.

I thought the worst thing anyone could call you was a cock-teaser. So, if you flirted, you had to be prepared to go through with it. Sleeping with someone was perfectly normal once you had done it. You didn't really worry about it. But there were other problems. The problems had to do with something else entirely.

*

Mack was during the hottest summer ever recorded. We were renting a house on an island with all sorts of other people. No one slept during the heat wave, walking around the house with nothing on which we were used to because of the nude beach. In the living room, Eddie lay on top of a coffee table to cool off. Mack and I, with the bedroom door open for air, sweated and sweated all night.

"I can't take this," he said at three A.M. "I'm going for a swim." He and some guys down the hall went to the beach. The heat put me on edge. I sat on a cracked chest by the open window and smoked and smoked till I felt even worse, waiting for something — I guess for him to get back.

One was on a camping trip in Colorado. We zipped our sleeping bags together, the coyotes' hysterical chatter far away. Other couples murmured in other tents. Paul was up before sunrise, starting a fire for breakfast. He wasn't much of a talker in the daytime. At night, his hand leafed about in the hair at my neck.

There'd be times when you overdid it. You'd get carried away. All the next day, you'd be in a total fog, delirious, absent-minded, crossing the street and nearly getting run over.

The more girls a boy has, the better. He has a bright look, having reaped fruits, blooming. He

10

stalks around, sure-shouldered, and you have the feeling he's got more in him, a fatter heart, more stories to tell. For a girl, with each boy it's as though a petal gets plucked each time.

Then you start to get tired. You begin to feel diluted, like watered-down stew.

Oliver came skiing with us. We lolled by the fire after everyone had gone to bed. Each creak you'd think was someone coming downstairs. The silver loop bracelet he gave me had been a present from his girlfriend before.

On vacations, we went skiing, or you'd go south if someone invited you. Some people had apartments in New York that their families hardly ever used. Or summer houses, or older sisters. We always managed to find someplace to go.

We made the plan at coffee hour. Simon snuck out and met me at Main Gate after lights-out. We crept to the chapel and spent the night in the balcony. He tasted like onions from a submarine sandwich.

The boys are one of two ways: either they can't sit still or they don't move. In front of the TV, they won't budge. On weekends they play touch football while we sit on the sidelines, picking blades of grass to chew on, and watch. We're always watching them run around. We shiver in the stands, knocking our boots together to keep our toes warm, and they whizz across the ice, chopping their sticks around the puck. When they're in the rink, they refuse to look at you, only eyeing each other beneath low helmets. You cheer for them but they don't look up, even if it's a face-off when nothing's happening, even if they're doing drills before any game has started at all.

Dancing under the pink tent, he bent down and whispered in my ear. We slipped away to the lawn on the other side of the hedge. Much later, as he was leaving the buffet with two plates of eggs and sausage, I saw the grass stains on the knees of his white pants.

Tim's was shaped like a banana, with a graceful curve to it. They're all different. Willie's like a bunch of walnuts when nothing was happening, another's as thin as a thin hot dog. But it's like faces; you're never really surprised.

Still, you're not sure what to expect.

I look into his face and he looks back. I look into his eyes and they look back at mine. Then they look down at my mouth so I look at his mouth, then back to his eyes then, backing up, at his whole face. I think, Who? Who are you? His head tilts to one side.

I say, "Who are you?"

"What do you mean?"

"Nothing."

I look at his eyes again, deeper. Can't tell who he is, what he thinks.

"What?" he says. I look at his mouth.

"I'm just wondering," I say and go wandering across his face. Study the chin line. It's shaped like a persimmon.

"Who are you? What are you thinking?"

He says, "What the hell are you talking about?"

Then they get mad after, when you say enough is enough. After, when it's easier to explain that you don't want to. You wouldn't dream of saying that maybe you weren't really ready to in the first place.

Gentle Eddie. We waded into the sea, the waves round and plowing in, buffalo-headed, slapping our thighs. I put my arms around his freckled shoulders and he held me up, buoyed by the water, and rocked me like a sea shell.

I had no idea whose party it was, the apartment jam-packed, stepping over people in the hallway. The room with the music was practically empty, the bare floor, me in red shoes. This fellow slides onto one knee and takes me around the waist and we rock to jazzy tunes, with my toes pointing heaven-ward, and waltz and spin and dip to "Smoke Gets in Your Eyes" or "I'll Love You Just for Now." He puts his head to my chest, runs a sweeping hand down my inside thigh and we go loose-limbed and sultry and as smooth as silk and I stamp my red heels and he takes me into a swoon. I never saw him again after that but I thought, I could have loved that one.

You wonder how long you can keep it up. You begin to feel as if you're showing through, like a bathroom window that only lets in grey light, the kind you can't see out of.

They keep coming around. Johnny drives up at Easter vacation from Baltimore and I let him in the kitchen with everyone sound asleep. He has friends waiting in the car.

"What are you, crazy? It's pouring out there," I say.

"It's okay," he says. "They understand."

So he gets some long kisses from me, against the refrigerator, before he goes because I hate those girls who push away a boy's face as if she were made out of Ivory soap, as if she's that much greater than he is.

The note on my cubby told me to see the headmaster. I had no idea for what. He had received complaints about my amorous displays on the town green. It was Willie that spring. The headmaster told me he didn't care what I did but that Casey Academy had a reputation to uphold in the town. He lowered his glasses on his nose. "We've got twenty acres of woods on this campus," he said. "If you want to smooch with your boyfriend, there are twenty acres for you to do it out of the public eye. You read me?"

Everybody'd get weekend permissions for different places, then we'd all go to someone's house whose parents were away. Usually there'd be more boys than girls. We raided the liquor closet and smoked pot at the kitchen table and you'd never know who would end up where, or with whom. There were always disasters. Ceci got bombed and cracked her head open on the banister and needed stitches. Then there was the time Wendel Blair walked through the picture window at the Lowes' and got slashed to ribbons.

He scared me. In bed, I didn't dare look at him. I lay back with my eyes closed, luxuriating because he knew all sorts of expert angles, his hands never fumbling, going over my whole body, pressing the hair up and off the back of my head, giving an extra hip shove, as if to say *There*. I parted my eyes slightly, keeping the screen of my lashes low because it was too much to look at him, his mouth loose and pink and parted, his eyes looking through my forehead, or kneeling up, looking

15

through my throat. I was ashamed but couldn't look him in the eye.

You wonder about things feeling a little off-kilter. You begin to feel like a piece of pounded veal.

At boarding school, everyone gets depressed. We go in and see the housemother, Mrs. Gunther. She got married when she was eighteen. Mr. Gunther was her high school sweetheart, the only boyfriend she ever had.

"And you knew you wanted to marry him right off?" we ask her.

She smiles and says, "Yes."

"They always want something from you," says Jill, complaining about her boyfriend.

"Yeah," says Giddy. "You always feel like you have to deliver something."

"You do," says Mrs. Gunther. "Babies."

After sex, you curl up like a shrimp, something deep inside you ruined, slammed in a place that sickens at slamming, and slowly you fill up with an overwhelming sadness, an elusive gaping worry. You don't try to explain it, filled with the knowledge that it's nothing after all, everything filling up finally and absolutely with death. After the brisk-ness of loving, loving stops. And you roll over with death stretched out alongside you like a feather boa, or a snake, light as air, and you . . . you don't even ask for anything or try to say something to him because it's obviously your own damn fault. You haven't been able to — to what? To open your heart. You open your legs but can't, or don't dare anymore, to open your heart.

It starts this way:

You stare into their eyes. They flash like all the stars are out. They look at you seriously, their eyes at a low burn and their hands no matter what starting off shy and with such a gentle touch that the only thing you can do is take that tenderness and let yourself be swept away. When, with one attentive finger they tuck the hair behind your ear, you —

You do everything they want.

Then comes after. After when they don't look at you. They scratch their balls, stare at the ceiling. Or if they do turn, their gaze is altogether changed. They are surprised. They turn casually to look at you, distracted, and get a mild distracted surprise. You're gone. Their blank look tells you that the girl they were fucking is not there anymore. You seem to have disappeared.

Sparks

OKAY, SO I MET this guy the other night.

I can just hear Duer saying — if I ever told him — *That's great.* Can just hear it, all the way from California after he's gone into the other room and shut the door so she can't hear. I can picture him exactly — his sneakers up on the desk, wearing shorts, acting as if he's having a perfectly normal conversation even though it's me. Out the window are the palm trees they have out there, the round and bristling kind that look as if they've had the living daylights scared out of them, but he's not looking at them. Instead he is lifting his shirt, keeping the phone tucked by his chin, to see if he's getting fat.

Whoever she is anyway.

But the other night I did meet this guy. I don't know. I mean I didn't know *what*. It got me rattled. He was an actor, okay? with cheekbones and a chin and this direct soulful gaze, and I thought *forget this*. Needless to say . . .

The only reason I went in the first place was Stacey. I made lame excuses. She said, "It's just dinner at Jenny's, Lil," using her fed-up-sister voice. "You're coming."

Half of Jenny's penthouse is an art gallery. Voices were coming from the kitchen so we walked in and right off I saw him, this guy in black pants and boots, talking to Jenny. His hips were at a certain angle, a curious face. I couldn't look. We gave kisses to Nita and Lex, smiling with their suntans — Lex had on a faded green shirt he'd been wearing since high school and around Nita's throat hung her usual gold chain with the charm and the dangling fist. Duer wears a chain, a plain one. Out of the corner of my eye was the guy leaning to look at Jenny's earring, she with her jaw tilted up. His profile was interested — it unnerved me — was he *really* interested? I escaped into the gallery.

The walls were white. In one corner was a fellow covered in chalk. We pretended we weren't aware of each other and looked at the pictures: scowling teenagers with smoke drifting from their mouths. A famous writer, scowling. Trees in Central Park in the dead of winter looking like nerve explosions. New York pictures. One of a girl in an empty bathtub had her giggling, the man's shirt on her unbuttoned all the way down. From what I hear of Duer, he has girls like that, one after another, undoing them like buttons.

We sat on the floor. The only piece of furniture was a square red leather chair and Stacey was in it. The lilac barrettes in her hair matched the lilac colors of her skirt; things on Stacey usually matched. So in walked the guy holding his beer bottle with two fingers, Mr. Casual, strolling in not the least bit self-conscious at all. Stacey was finding out things, like that the fellow with the dust was a carpenter from Brooklyn but a sculptor really. Another fellow in a tie and blazer as if this were a real dinner party had three names. One of them was Pierpont. Jenny had shrugged and said he was just a friend of the family. The actor, it turned out, had just made a movie. Stacey asked him about that. He launched into a detailed plot explanation.

Duer says, "Maybe I'll try the movies," half kidding but really not kidding at all.

"But you can't act."

"You don't have to," he says, meaning he has the looks. We go to the movies a lot — we see the one about the woman psychiatrist who has her own nervous breakdown and after when I'm dissolving again, he says, "I told you we shouldn't have seen that one."

Everyone tilted forward politely, listening. In the middle of the floor like a centerpiece were Stacey's red plastic shoes and during pauses in the conversation we'd look at them. The guy had a lot to say, sitting there with his boots crossed at the ankles, cheerful, clasping his knees. He was talking about his bike being stolen. His face darkened for a moment, then, as fast, became bright again.

The carpenter muttered so we could barely hear. "We all get burned," I think he said.

There was one ashtray and I leaned over to it and suddenly the guy is two inches from my face, asking me, close up, "What do you do?" He was good-looking, all right? and it was too obvious. He had this eager, obvious expression. It's trouble when they're handsome, I'm not kidding.

I asked did anyone want another beer and fled to the kitchen.

At a party Duer walks straight up to the best-looking girl and plants himself an inch away from her. Or at a restaurant if he sees a girl going by, he'll bolt out in pursuit, his napkin in his hand. After she disappears he stops, out of breath in the freezing cold, laughing, tapping his cowboy boots, letting the other girls get a good look at him.

"You could not believe it," Nita was saying and Lex finished her sentence, "There were fifteen bridesmaids." They watched Jenny shake lettuce at the sink; her shorts reached to the backs of her knees.

"You're kidding," Jenny said, not surprised. Jenny acts as if everything is perfectly regular.

24

"Her dress had wings on it," Nita said.

"And there were fifteen ushers." Lex looked at Nita even though he was telling Jenny.

"You are kidding," Jenny said.

"Did her father give her away?" I asked and they all looked uncomfortable. Lex fidgeted with a corkscrew. The guy walked in, swiveling his head as if to ask why there was a dead silence.

"I'm sorry I'm such a black cloud," I say to Duer. He's gotten me out of bed for a walk by the Charles. The world, spring, is melting. I wear my nightgown under my beige coat and lean on his arm. The breeze bats itself mild over my face, feeling light and heavy at the same time.

"You are not a black cloud," he says.

"Oh I know . . . but I am. I really am a black cloud."

"You're not. Stop saying that."

The river is swollen and moving fast. "Isn't the air something?" I say and tears fill my eyes. Duer's face is close, listening.

"You are not a black cloud," he says after a while.

"But I don't believe . . . in this life . . ." I say and press my mouth against the corduroy of his sleeve to stop it and try to think of other things to say and try to keep breathing.

"To top it off," Nita was saying, fending off Lex at an arm's length, "we had to stay with his old girlfriend."

"We did not *have* to," Lex said, annoyed.

"Well we did."

"She's not even an old girlfriend," he said. "I went out with her when I was fourteen."

"Sixteen more like," Nita said and crossed the kitchen to stand next to Jenny. She watched her chop red peppers.

Lex headed for the door. "Whatever," he said.

Everyone drifted in and out. Stacey made a clatter searching for a pan. I found the beers in the freezer stacked like torpedoes.

The actor was saying to Jenny, "She moved out." He held his bottle at his hip like a pistol and stared angrily, suddenly in a sulk. Jenny nodded, counting napkins.

Duer has no problems whatsoever getting girls. His girlfriends are the types that flirt with waiters or who will dance with anyone who asks them, looking straight into the other person's eyes as if it were no big deal. Once at Café École a girl comes up to our table, hands Duer a note and leaves without a word. The note has her name and telephone number. He laughs and blushes and cranes out the window to see her cross the street. She's wearing bright red tights. Now, when he calls from California, he'll say, "I met this — ah — person," not daring to say *girl* to me. "Do I want to hear about it?" I say and wreck the conversation.

The guy had decided to explain his whole love life. He spoke to Jenny but everyone in there was listening. ". . . So wouldn't you think? After three years?"

"Sure," Jenny said matter-of-factly. She was banging a chicken with a wooden club.

"Not her. She won't speak to me."

"At all?" Nita said. This was her favorite topic of conversation, love difficulties.

The guy turned to her gratefully. "Don't you think that's strange?" Nita nodded and thoughtfully began picking at the label of her beer bottle.

Out the window above the sink I could see sluggish pleasure boats way out on the river. The water moved like lead, swirling and thick and opalescent. It was taking a long time to get dark.

"So now I've been going on dates," the guy was saying, "and they are the worst." I wandered out to the terrace where the carpenter was standing in the hot wind. He considered me from under his brow, expecting annoyance. I asked him how he knew Jenny. He'd been to college with her, he said, and now five years later had run into her coming out of a movie.

"Which one?" I asked, figuring I'd seen it.

"University of Montana," he said.

I heard the guy's voice reverberating in the kitchen. Duer always — no, forget it.

Typical actor — instead of remaining on the roof with the rest of us, he had to climb the water tower. Nita was shrieking at him, shrieking to be up on the roof in the first place. We'd gone up to see the sunset smudged with haze. The actor struck a pose like some swashbuckler, his shirt rippling in the wind. Lex crossed his arms and regarded the guy.

"Why don't you go up?" I asked.

"I'm chicken," he said proudly.

There was no guard wall. At the edge you could look past your toes to the street thirty stories below. Some kids were setting off firecrackers; they broke from a huddle. There were flashes, popping and crackling.

"Lil," Stacey said. I turned around. She was standing in the middle of the roof. "That's not funny," she said.

Jenny was showing the carpenter a pier that had burned for two days. Did you get any smoke? he asked softly. You're not kidding, Jenny said with no surprise in her voice. The guy on the water tower was pretending to fall, giving Nita a complete heart attack. Please! she screamed. I myself was wondering about the girl he mentioned, the one who wouldn't talk to him.

Then it was dark and we were the last ones left up there — me and Mr. Casual — he was chattering away about some book he'd just read, about astronauts and rockets. It was rigorous, he said, made him want to start boxing or something. You know? he said. I sort of nodded. Who was this guy? I could hardly make out his face in the dusk but when he gripped a sooty pipe right near me I could see his hand and something about his hand made me dizzy. Jesus. He told me he ran four miles a day. I wanted to tell him this didn't feel like a normal conversation, to tell him, I'm sorry, I'm not really normal, I'm —

"You're too hard on yourself," Duer says. He's watching himself in the mirror, putting on cologne, using mine.

"Hard on myself?" I give a pathetic laugh. I've got sweaters on and a shawl and around me is a sea of sheets. I haven't moved from bed for three months. It's like being stranded on an island, seasick.

He says maybe I should see the doctor again. "You can't take everything so seriously," he says. He rubs my knee under the covers like absentmindedly polishing a doorknob. Later, when he gets home from night classes, he kisses me and I taste beer.

There was a long thin whistle, then crackling, then way across the water we spotted the fireworks, way over New Jersey, so far away and so quiet, like flint being struck. They burst here and there like shifting artillery fire.

He came close. He leaned against the tar-black wall and his pants blended in. He apologized for being from California. The fireworks were recalling some childhood tragedy, a short circuit with Christmas lights. I pictured the holiday frazzle in the LA sun; he reimagined his own scene, staring off toward the river, his profile inches away in the dark. His mother still lived out there, he said, his voice going louder when he turned, which threw me off. What was that? I reached for the loop of the ladder to steady myself, wanting to explain, I haven't been well. My eyes felt hollow from trying to see in the dark and I stepped down the ladder, silently apologizing, shaky, one rung then the next, you see, I'm not completely —

"Come on," Duer says, long distance. "You're fine."

When I got to the bathroom I could hear Stacey and Jenny near the record player. "Lil seems fine," Jenny said in her regular voice.

"No," Stacey said, meaning *no* to something else, "she's much better."

I looked into the mirror to see if I could tell. When I put my fist to my chest, I could feel my heart up close to the skin like an ear up close listening at a door.

The chicken got burnt. "I think it's better that way," said the shy carpenter. The table was out on the terrace, curved glass tubes around the candles. The flames gave everyone animal eyes.

I sat next to him. I know it was brazen of me. I'm sure everyone noticed. I was perfectly nonchalant then suddenly felt utterly stupid, exposed. Not that he wasn't used to it, I'm sure, I'm sure it was perfectly normal for girls to seat themselves brazenly down, squaring their shoulders, settling their laps next to him. I banged my elbow and my fork went flying. Everyone politely ignored it. The actor, my dinner partner now, bent to retrieve it, twisting in his chair so that his black pants brushed against my leg.

"Whoops," he said in this eerie whisper.

The family friend in the tie and blazer, being conversational, said, "Jenny says you're a painter." I must have given him an odd look because he blushed behind his horn-rims. "Aren't you?"

Stacey said, "She is. And if she'd only do it more, she'd be good." Her eyes were warning me, her warning-sister eyes.

My dinner partner's plate was piled high with food. He hadn't touched it because he was talking so much. He cracked a joke. Everyone laughed. Nita kept laughing by leaving her mouth open, closing her eyes, and not making a sound. I was cutting my food. Suddenly he turned his chin my way. "Do you like to go dancing?" he said.

Eat your supper, I wanted to say, or Take me home and make me better, but instead I nodded and looked — I don't know — away.

Across the courtyard was an identical building with identical penthouses. The lights went on in one of them. Everyone hummed and nudged each other. This was going to be good, the window the size of a movie screen. It looked creepy over there, the light a weird topaz, the two people walking with bullet-shaped heads.

"Who is it?" Nita said and she leaned heavily against Lex. As if he'd know.

Jenny was picking cucumbers out of the salad bowl, not at all interested. "It's the bedroom," Lex said, which got even more hushed attention. Stacey had paused to look over her shoulder and her knife and fork were held in suspension over her plate.

Lying in bed, Duer and I can see the red neon sign across the river snaking forward like a fuse, blinking *COCA-COLA*.

He lit my cigarette. Not with a match like a normal person but with a whole candle, lifting it from the jumble of baskets and dishes and glasses, pretty damn suave, so the tube didn't wobble or make a sound. He held it. What could I say to that? How was I to respond?

I wake out of nightmares and Duer puts himself around me, holding my arms down, *Ssshhh*, he says as if he can hear the engine between my ears. Other times there are other sounds: wings flapping, as if a bird were trapped in my skull, or a distant throbbing, someone *else's* heart beating far off.

Mr. Entertainment was telling another story, about a bum in the back of a bus singing at the top of his lungs, booming out a baritone. We heard an imitation of it.

"My brother was a bum for a while," said the carpenter softly. "After his girlfriend left him. He used to sleep in front of church vents."

Stacey looked at me with a face that meant Uh-oh.

Duer isn't the type to worry. After school is out he takes me to Maine. He practically carries me to the car, my hair matted in an old braid, my face swollen. I talk a blue streak asking nonstop questions keeping the conversation going. He answers driving along perfectly normal, staring ahead.

That night in the middle of the night he comes into the bathroom with a towel around his waist.

"What is it?" he whispers. His eyes are in a tortured squint against the light.

I'm in the bathtub with my arms out over the edge, watching my hands dangle. "I think," I start but my voice is like static. I try again.

"What, Lil?" he says, begging, his hand clutching the towel in a fist.

"I think I've blown a fuse," I say.

In the morning, on the phone with Stacey, Duer holds my foot in his lap and touches it as if testing a peach for bruises. They discuss doctors; Duer looks at my perfectly calm face and his eyes glaze over. My own are as dry as sockets.

It's Stacey who drives me to the hospital. "I just want to rest," I tell her and saying it makes me start to shake like a car going over potholes. When I finally talk to Duer, four days later, I'm standing in the hall at the pay phone. In the background his record player is going pretty loud.

"I'm not supposed to come," he says. "They don't think it's a good idea."

Other patients are hanging around in the corridor trying to eavesdrop. "They don't?" I say.

I hear him bite into something like a carrot. He says he's still going to California for law school. "I know, Duer," I say. As if I've forgotten that. Then I simply don't see him again. The other person who doesn't visit is my father, but he doesn't know what to do either.

Jenny got up. "Prepare yourselves," she said in her deadpan way, "for a surprise dessert."

"Goodie," Nita said, eying Lex as if she'd like to eat him.

We carried the dishes into the bright kitchen. Jenny ordered us, "Get out," waving us away. "Just sit out there and wait."

"Okay, okay," laughed the actor, his hands fluttering up near his ears.

The one time that Jenny comes to the hospital with Stacey, she asks me, "Are you getting shock?" Direct question. I've brought her into the bathroom so we can smoke. Her cigarette pack has a bull's-eye on it.

"Why, do I look it?"

"No," she says, puffing away, perfectly comfortable leaning against some washroom sink.

"But I have to talk to the doctor," I say. "Which is worse."

The doctor wants to know about Duer. He peers down from a height. I look small to him, a wreck. He wants to know — sex, obviously. He wants to know how old I was.

"Fifteen."

"That's quite young, isn't it?"

"Maybe."

"What did your parents say?"

"To what?"

He is specifically blunt, trying to shock me.

I say, "That was hardly a topic of conversation."

"I see," he says, taking in a distant landscape.

"No," I say. "My father wouldn't ever say anything. He'd let Mum handle it."

"And what did she say?"

She whispers through the crack that it's time for church and Duer freezes under my quilt. She is gentle, a gentle mother, shutting the door. "Did she see me?" he whispers, his face appearing with the covers like a kerchief. His body is a huge lump in the bed and I give him this look. "What do you think?" I say.

I tell the doctor, "Nothing."

"And the time you had that trouble?"

By now I'm sick of this and exhausted. "Which time?" I ask him back.

"What the hell is she doing in there?" Lex said, listening for something in the kitchen.

"Cool your jets," Nita said.

"Patience, patience," muttered the carpenter happily, a little drunk.

The fellow in the tie tried to brighten the conversation. "Has anyone seen the movie about — ?"

Then right in my ear this guy started whispering maybe we should all go dancing somewhere or maybe he and I could get a — I looked down and watched his hands pick apart one of the little carnations Jenny had in the vase, his fingers slowly and deliberately shredding the whole thing. Or else, he was saying, I could get your number —

It was too much; I panicked. "What are you doing?" I said, interrupting him and trying to joke the way someone else might, pointing to the flower to tease him.

His face jerked away as if he'd been stung and a rash spread down around his eyes and his cheeks went haggard. My own face dropped, idiotic and speechless and ashamed. He had dropped the ruined flower to pick his fingernails and was staring at the rim of his wineglass, thinking of something else entirely.

The blood came roaring up past my ears and darkened my vision. I tried to stand up but the dizziness got worse. Suddenly out of nowhere everyone was roaring and hooting. I gripped the table and managed to push myself up into that loud, mottled air. Something bright flashed in front of me; there was a hissing and gentle flames and Jenny's startled eyes.

I almost knocked her over. She was holding the dessert platter high as if it had taken flight. The baked apples on it started to roll and in my daze I saw one go over the edge and then it thumped, still aflame, like a beanbag onto me. Embers stuck. Everyone shot up and flapped around and batted at it. I couldn't remember the last time I'd been flapped over, much less handled at all, so when two hands fastened onto my upper arms I didn't think of what I was saying — with all this trying to stand up, trying to connect, trying to put out sparks — and just exploded with, "Duer —"

I know. But that's what came out.

The hands let go and I was plopped back in my chair. The bustling settled and went quiet. Stacey's face appeared concerned in front of me, looking this way and that, assessing from different angles.

Jenny said, "So much for pommes flambées." She picked up the fallen apple and lobbed it over the terrace wall.

"Did it burn through?" Nita whispered with fascination and her head came close. Over her shoulder I noticed the lights, noticed the city for the first time all night, the dots zigzagging everywhere. There was a yellow glow like you get from a bonfire. Nita's hand hovered over the singed place on my shirt, feeling for heat. In the candlelight Stacey was thoughtfully pressing the base of her wineglass, turning it slightly, adjusting it. Behind her the tiny lights dazzled, flung like sequins across the dark blocks. In each window, a TV probably, with snowy reception or a radio picking up airwaves, crackling like me, and beside the icebox vent a bowl of cat food set out, waiting. Lex said something about still hoping for the dessert anyway. Jenny brought the coffee cups all shaky across the terrace. In the opposite apartment the lights had gone out and the windows were dark like dark mirrors. It's always seemed odd to me, and wrong, that the lights far away are the ones which sparkle most quickly, flickering, like the currents of the heart, the distant tremblings felt more urgently sometimes than the ones near at hand. The quiet carpenter, hunched, struck a match and held it lingeringly to his cigarette. Jenny spooned out the apples and the hum going around the table was low and appreciative. Then he — the guy — got up.

He was leaving. His metal chair scratched the brick when he pushed it back and he stood up, preparing to go. I didn't look.

His hands pressed the back of his chair. "I wish I could stay," he lied, "but I have to be heading." He switched boots. "Time to hit the road." Some cowboy pulling out of town.

There was a sigh and everybody's shoulders rose up a little. No one wanted him to go. *Awwww*, they said. For an instant he looked as if he might change his mind, reclaim his chair, have another beer to please his audience or maybe a little more — he took in all the rosy faces — wine. Seeing mine no doubt decided him. To protect myself against further shock, I was concentrating all my attention on a flame's stray flirtation with a mild draft. He left.

I reached for Stacey's lit cigarette, the rattle mounting again, took a second nervous drag then looked for one of my own, knowing I'd done wrong again and sorry for it. I went for the candle, which despite the glass tube had — served me right — gone out.

I sank back exhausted and inside the apartment heard the elevator humming down with the guy in it. I fumbled the cigarette at my lips, quite ashamed of myself, when suddenly there was a mild glow from all these matches being struck and all these arms came forward, each cupping a tiny flame. They'd been there all along and were only waiting — five, even six — so all I had to do whether I deserved it or not was to lean forward into their light, my cheeks ablaze, and take my pick.

Blow

He called in the middle of the day to ask if he could come over. Two minutes later he was at the door, eleven flights up. He jumped back when I opened the door, startled, sort of shielding himself with his briefcase. "Bill," I said.

He craned his neck inside to check if anyone were hiding by the door hinges. He was wearing a nice dark suit and a clean white shirt. His face was as pale as chalk, his eyes pink-rimmed.

"Come on in."

"Helen and I broke up this weekend," he said. "I haven't slept in three days."

"God, Bill."

He circled into the small kitchen. He was like a hunted man. "I just need someplace till my doctor's appointment. It's at three-thirty." He was picking up things on the shelves, the little spice jars, the honey. "I'll just keep doing coke till then."

"What if you stopped?"

He eyed me. "I'd really be in trouble. I'd be dangerous." I've known Bill for a long time. For months we might not see each other, or even a year. But it never seems like that.

"I brought you some things." He handed me a plastic shopping bag. On top were books. I took them out. "You read French, don't you?" Bill said.

I laughed. "Not really."

"Oh, I thought you read French." He doesn't crack a smile. "The other one is about childhood, because you write about childhood."

"Thanks, Bill. Thanks."

Next are a pair of men's trousers from a vintage clothes store. I hold them up. "Nice," I say.

He's nodding with a serious expression. "They look good on."

Last is a vest, grey-striped with satin backing. "It might be big," he says. "But it was the best one."

I try it on. "Vests can't be too big."

"It's to keep you warm." He spun around. "You go back to work if you want." He pointed fiercely to my desk.

"It's all right," I say. I don't tell him I wasn't getting anything done anyway. I ask him if he wants some tea.

"Do you have fruit? Something with potassium in it."

I opened the icebox. Pretty bare. I hadn't been buying much food lately.

"Like bananas," Bill said.

"What about yogurt? It's got bananas in it."

Bill took the carton and had one bite. "I've lost ten pounds," he said. "Can I use your phone?" He left the yogurt on the stove. "Denise, hi. It's me." Bill looked at my face but through me. "He did? What'd you tell him? Good. Then messenger over the affidavit. What? Tomorrow." There was some commotion out in the hall. Bill glanced at me with terror. "Wait. I'll call you later." He hung up. "What's that?"

"Some people getting off the elevator."

"I don't want anyone to know I'm here."

"No one's coming, Bill."

"What about your roommate?"

"She's at work."

"Don't tell her I was here, okay?" He sat down then sprang up again, pacing. "She's a friend of Helen's. I don't want Helen to feel guilty about me."

"Okay, but —"

"If she asks"— Bill gave me an odd look —"tell her your lover was here."

I smile at that. He sees it, looks angry. "Who was that guy you were with the other night anyway?"

"Well actually, that was." I know I'm grinning but can't stop it.

"He was very rude to me."

"He was?" This surprises me.

"He didn't introduce himself *and* he knocked my drink over." Bill was going through his pockets, picking out tiny pieces of paper.

"But I introduced you."

"He didn't," Bill said.

"On the couch," I said. "Remember?"

Bill shook his head. "I didn't like the look of him."

"No?"

Bill was concentrating on unfolding a sort of origami thing. "What's he do?"

"D.P. You know, cinematographer." It gives me a thrill saying it.

"Those guys are weird," Bill said.

"They are?" He was sniffing from a cut-off straw, didn't notice me beaming.

"They like to control people," he said, holding his breath in. "Men can tell these things about other men. I'm telling you, that guy was not all there."

Later we decided to go to the museum. I don't usually take the afternoon off but work didn't seem so pressing.

Bill took me to a part of the museum I'd never really seen, the Islamic art. No one else was in there. There was one room with inlaid marble, a fountain, gold palms on the wall. It was quiet and mysterious with the sound of trickling water. He told me all this outlandish stuff about Persia — fertility rites, hunting accidents, stories of monsters. There were a lot of nightmares and heads being chopped off. I don't know where he got it all from, the coke probably. He had an intense, humorless delivery, talking on about the orgies. He used to be such an easygoing guy, Bill. A long time ago we almost got together — a few times, now that I think about it — but for some reason it never worked out.

He eyed me suspiciously. He didn't think I was listening to him. His eyelids were pink with anger.

Bill said a lot of stuff that day, upset by everything. Near the end, it began to wear on me. But I couldn't feel too bad. I was in that stage of being in love when you're up in the clouds, out of it, feeling no pain. I nodded at Bill, smiled. He went on, more stuff about Persia, more about the cinematographer. I wasn't believing a word of it.

Later when I came down I found out all of it was true.

City Night

"YOU'RE RIGHT HERE," said her host, singling out Ellen and patting the cushion beside him. In her twenty-seven years Ellen Greenough had managed to steer clear of this sort of fellow, enormously pleased with himself, always having a splendid time. The boys she knew were thoughtful types, a little wistful and perplexed. When they gazed into her eyes she had the uneasy feeling that what they wanted most was to be taken care of.

She weaved through the mismatched chairs and benches and strangers, feeling how long it had been since she'd been to a dinner party. For the past three years she'd been at home in New England looking after her dying mother. Afterward, Ellen had moved to New York, staying with her mother's friend, Mrs. Means, while she looked for an apartment. Tina Means, the daughter, was a journalist and had known Ellen since they were young. Tina had brought her to this party tonight.

A white tablecloth partly camouflaged the different heights of the tables beneath. Candles gave off the only glow of light. Guests sidled into their seats lackadaisically, many having been here before. The chatter was a din.

Nicholas Dickson, the host, was the last to sit down. He wore a loose white shirt and a mild satisfied expression, surveying the table, making sure everything was taken care of. Ellen noticed a small ponytail she'd not seen before. Tina had known Nicholas Dickson a long time. "He's a great guy," she'd said through her cigarette smoke. "Watch out." Ellen only vaguely understood.

"So tell me," he said, his voice calm in the clatter, "what you do." He gazed at her with a rapt expression, ignoring his food.

Ellen told him she was a student.

"Wait, don't tell me." Nicholas Dickson smiled, his teeth as white as his shirt. It was a game and he liked games. "Literature?" Ellen shook her head. "Theatre?" She couldn't tell how ironic he was being. "Not another journalist?" he said, shielding one eye.

"Nothing glamorous," she said. "Art history."

"Oh, but that is glamorous," he said. His expression seemed to melt. "I love art history." He took up his knife and fork. "Tell me your favorite thing."

"Actually, I'm learning to be a restorer."

"Really? Good for you." He began talking about artists he knew, calling them by their first names. So-and-so's dealer was there. He gestured loosely down the table. Ellen began to ask him what exactly it was that he did but his attention was snatched up by a woman at the end of the table.

"Nicky!" she screeched, toying with a clattering necklace. It looked like the contents of a tool box, grey and sharp. "What was the name of that model? The one who dragged us out to Connecticut."

Nicholas Dickson's memory was decidedly more fond for he smiled serenely. "Evalina," he said, not raising his voice.

"God! That's right!" the woman cried and burrowed back into her conversation.

Throughout the meal, Nicholas Dickson leaned toward Ellen, listening to her with an amused expression. Of course, he did have to make sure the salad got around, that the wineglasses stayed full, and then the dessert did need organizing . . . eventually he abandoned his seat altogether.

Sitting on Ellen's right was a well-dressed fellow with a stickpin in his tie. His name was Theo. By the end of the meal, Theo had turned sideways and was holding his face an inch from Ellen's, his knees pressed primly together. His gaze wandered drunkenly around the room.

"Why, I ask you, are all the women madly in love with Nicholas Dickson?" he whispered.

"Are they?"

Theo nodded. "All he has to do is look at a girl and she'll jump into bed with him." His tone was thick and forlorn.

"Really?" To Ellen, this seemed unlikely.

Theo's eyebrows met in a point, sad but true. Then he frowned, trying to focus on ice cream melting on a plate. "I don't understand it. He's not that handsome. Look at him." Nicholas Dickson was nowhere in sight. "But he's a wonderful friend to me." Theo turned his brimming eyes to Ellen. "Men know how to be friends." He seemed to notice Ellen for the first time. "But how would you know? You're too young. How old are you anyway? God, you're just a baby."

"Can I get you something else?" whispered the gentle voice in her ear. "Is there anything you need?" Ellen turned around. Nicholas Dickson was crouched at the back of her chair, holding on, his shoulders filling out the rounded sides of his shirt.

"No," she said. She could feel the warmth coming off him. "Thanks. I'm fine."

"Some cognac? More wine?"

"Really. I'm perfect."

"I have to make sure all my guests are happy."

"I'm sure they are."

"I hope you've been having a fun time."

"Oh yes. Theo has been quite informative."

"Really," he said. "How unlike Theo."

"Yes, he's been talking about you."

The golden look vanished from his face and his profile turned, soldier-like, to some dim figures collapsed on a couch. "Excuse me," he said and was gone.

There was a movement to head downtown. People scrambled through the piles of overcoats, put on gloves and hats. Ellen had no intention of going with them — she had an early class — but down on the sidewalk among the milling shadows, Nicholas Dickson gripped her elbow in an oddly commanding way, staring ahead, and there was no question of her not going. As they waited for a cab, he took a scarf from around his neck and wrapped it under Ellen's face, tucking at her chin. The scarf was black and soft. With his touch, the will seemed to drain out of her and she had the dependent feeling of a child being dressed for the cold.

The cab stopped on a crosstown street in front of a windowless building. A small cluster of people huddled in the cold. Feet stomped gently, breath rose in the spotlight. Behind the roped-off sidewalk three dim figures leaned against a shiny black door, unimpressed.

Nicholas Dickson glided from the car into the

crowd with a serious expression. This was serious business. His arm rose and pointed to the heads in his party. The entourage filed by solemnly, lingering just inside the door. Nicholas Dickson peeled back some bills, rosy in the lamplight, and paid for them all.

They passed through a heavy red curtain into a large room where brass fixtures gleamed in the distance and a beaded chandelier glistened like a huge evening pouch. Opera played. Dark heads turned from a polished bar, watching them walk in.

A white-skinned woman in décolletage threw back her head. She nuzzled one shoulder, flung an arm into the air. "Gorgeous," she said, dropping her wrist and dimpling her cheeks. An expert gaze snapped Ellen like a shutter. She curled around Nicholas Dickson's arm, commenting on the evening's clientele. Ellen was flashed a smile.

They drifted, they sat. Now they were upstairs curved into a red booth, the group of them, Theo swaying and muttering, Tina Means lighting cigarettes with gusto. People came and went — exuberant greetings, moments without a word. Then they were downstairs slumped on a couch, music thumping in the next room. They did not dance. A porcelain-faced fellow perched on the arm of a velvet sofa, chatted languidly, fluttered away. Nicholas Dickson leaned close to Ellen and whispered, "The only reason I'm here is you."

Vacant faces passed, tall figures, hollow cheeks.

Who were they all? Nicholas Dickson surveyed the crowd, chin raised, pleased. A handsome fellow crouched at his knee, involving him in a secret discussion.

Ellen held a drink in her hand and thought dully of her morning class. That world was very far away.

Not that she felt anymore in this world — sitting in a smoky room with a ridiculous drink in her hand. She looked down at it. It was melting. Something flashed in her mind: her mother's fist against a white bedspread, squeezing itself against pain.

The night flapped on, disoriented and dark. Ellen had given up trying to steer herself through it. Sitting beside Nicholas Dickson, she felt like something washed ashore after a shipwreck.

"I'm not sure I know how to behave in a nightclub," he said. She regarded him. He looked different for a moment — something real appeared.

"No," she said.

He stood up. "Then let's go."

She let herself be swept along. She didn't want to think. They passed through more curtains. He knew where to go.

Outside the heavy doors it was still and cold. Streetlights threw down a harsh glare. Wayward figures still lingered impossibly by the door. Limos sent up white flags of exhaust. Ellen felt a hand toy with the hair at the back of her neck. "Roommate home tonight?" he said.

Ellen smiled uncertainly.

He turned her to face him, holding her shoulders. He kissed her. Oh, she thought, my. Her heart stopped then started off again, faster.

"I think you better come home with me," he said in a close, husky voice. His arms were around her, their coats bulky between them.

"I don't think that's such a good idea," she said, but her eyes were glittering.

"You don't?" he teased and tucked at the scarf. It was there after all. "Why not?" He turned to signal for a cab, holding on to her, not letting her go.

"It's dangerous," she said.

"What is?"

"People," she said, ducking blankly into the back seat. "Other people."

"Me especially," said Nicholas Dickson. He gave the driver his address then settled Ellen back against the seat, arranging himself around her. He felt very warm. They rode uptown in silence.

And silently they climbed his four flights, the same stairs of hours before, only now it was more solemn and they were shy. She stood near him while he rattled the locks, already with other things on his mind.

He led her by the arm through the dark shadows of the dinner, keeping the lights off. She saw a tiny red light blinking on an answering machine. He sat her on the bed. The light went on in the bathroom, making a rectangle of light at her feet. She saw novels, travel books, then the light went out.

He was beside her, kissing her gently. She felt as if she were somewhere else. "Let's get this off," he said breathlessly and pulled back her coat in a gesture so smooth it nearly knocked the wind out of her. He pressed close. She felt as if she were setting off for a place she'd only vaguely heard about. Her heart was going madly, knowing nothing, feeling no pain.

He was taking all her air. She fell back, drowning, then she slipped into that unconsciousness when the struggle is let go of and death becomes a welcome thing.

It was brittle and raw in the morning when they stepped onto the deserted sidewalk. The avenue was grey. A cab appeared from out of nowhere and screeched to a halt. Nicholas Dickson tucked Ellen inside and clipped shut the door. His eyebrows rose, jauntily fighting the exhaustion in his eyes, his hand fluttered up in a wave. The cab took off and he turned abruptly, clutching his collar beneath his chin.

The cab lurched forward, hurling Ellen back against the seat. She hardly noticed, half focusing on the buildings whizzing by. She made a vague attempt to register what was coming over her — the strange night, the strange man, what she'd seen. She felt strangely afloat. It wasn't love. One did not fall in love with men like Nicholas Dickson. That's what Tina Means would say. She smiled at the thought, an ironic smile, not the sort of smile Ellen had ever smiled before. She could feel the difference.

They stopped at a light. Out in the frigid morning a group of children were waiting for their bus. Mothers were fidgeting with zippers. One woman stood with a patient face, rubbing a little hooded figure leaning against her thigh, warming the both of them. The cab bounded forward.

That was one world. Then there was her work, another world. She still had time to make her morning class but wouldn't bother. Did it matter? You let things matter then you lost them and where were you then?

She'd seen a new world, one she didn't know anything about. She was drawn to it. In that world, it seemed, one did not need to care.

TWO

Lunch with Harry

THE TWO WOMEN bustled into the restaurant from off the rainy street. "Jane!" cried the taller of them, scolding.

The small woman shook out her umbrella, laughing. "That's nothing." She ruffled the back of her hair. It was shiny as mink, cut fashionably off her neck. "How ridiculously late are we?" She checked her mascara with the back of her wrist. "Do you see him, Emma?"

Emma scanned the dining room. She had a tranquil face and pale hair. The glow of the wall lights reflected in the horizontal mirrors above the banquettes. "Not here," she said. She had a European accent and rolled her *r*'s.

The maître d' appeared darkly before them.

"Nasty out there." Jane smiled. She tugged at her narrow skirt, straightening it.

"Harry Loder," Emma said placidly.

"Right this way."

The man slid out of the back booth when he spotted the women. He was a broad-shouldered man with hair reaching to his collar. He wore a well-cut suit, no tie. His top button was buttoned maybe a little tight.

"Here you are," he said, embracing Emma. He had an accent, too, a British one. Emma took the hug happily, going limp. Harry gazed at her. "Wonderful Emma," he said, pulling out the table while she inched along the cushioned curve, looking about.

"Hi," Jane said. "Sorry we're late." She sprung up to kiss him. "Whoops, I've left a mark." She reached up and rubbed his chin. Harry held the back of her chair. "There," she said and sat down.

Harry slid in beside Emma. "So you made it," he said fondly.

"Poor Emma," Jane said, removing her gloves, checking her earrings. "I've been dragging her through this storm. For some reason I thought it was off Lex, so we let the cab go. Isn't that stupid, I don't know what I was thinking, I —"

"Well you're here now," Harry said, watching Emma.

"It's nice here," Emma said.

64

"Harry's hangout," Jane said. "Don't you think Emma should move here, Harry? I've been trying to convince her." Their faces turned toward Emma.

Harry's eyes ticked back and forth, impatient for the waiter. "She should, of course." His expression softened when he looked at Emma.

The waiter handed out menus. "Wine," Jane said. "Definitely wine."

"Emma wants some oysters, doesn't she?" Harry said.

Emma nodded, holding her menu loosely, not reading it.

"Any soup?" Jane said. "I need to warm these bones."

The waiter took their orders and left.

Jane made tiny adjustments to the silverware. "Any word, Harry?" she said, rubbing the table-cloth.

"No."

"That is a bore," Emma said.

Harry shrugged uncomfortably. "What can you do?"

"Nothing?" Jane said. "Wait." She leaned toward Emma. "They'll be crazy if they don't take it. It's really the best thing he's done." Harry frowned, not wanting to listen.

Emma nodded, gazed dreamily about the room, her eyes like dark round buttons. "There are the murals you mentioned," she said.

"Yes, there they are." Harry turned as much as the booth and his size allowed. "So tell me about the party. Have you been having a fabulous time?"

"Fred and Stephanie had a wonderful singer there," Emma said.

"Really?"

"Tell him about the dress," Jane said.

"It was wonderful. No back at all, with lots of feathers everywhere. She had a wonderful voice too. I loved her."

"Sounds — well, wonderful."

"I saw Rachel there," Emma said.

"Really," said Harry with a blank look.

"Your old flame?" Jane said casually, not quite carrying it off.

The wine arrived. Harry tasted it.

"Wasn't she?" Jane mouthed to Emma. Emma nodded. "Sort of." They all watched the wine being poured.

"I think Fred and Stephanie have a strange marriage," Emma said.

"Do you?" Harry broke his bread with two hands and buttered it.

"When do they ever see each other?"

"They seem to get along fine," Harry said. "I'm sure they're wonderfully happy."

"He has all those assistants in his studio. They're all beautiful young girls," Emma said.

"Lucky Fred. How wonderful for him."

"Not so wonderful for Stephanie I shouldn't think."

"I shouldn't think so either," Jane said, sipping her soup.

Henry looked down at Jane for the first time. "But you don't know them. So it's pointless to say."

"True," Jane said. Her head remained bowed. "But I know what people are like."

"Europeans are different from Americans," he said with a stiff grin.

"So you say."

"Anyway." Harry took an expansive breath. "I think Stephanie is smart. Let him have his little flirtations. Then he'll always come back to her."

"Unless of course he doesn't," Emma said.

"What about the humiliation?" Jane said.

"Women shouldn't ask for what they know they can't get," Harry said matter-of-factly. "That's the mistake they make."

Jane frowned a little. She caught sight of her reflection in the mirror and immediately made her expression smooth.

For dessert, Harry offered the women bites of his chocolate cake. They both shook their heads vehemently. Glancing at his watch, Harry excused himself to make a phone call.

"He does seem worried," Emma said.

Jane picked up his fork and began finishing his dessert. "I'm not helping much."

"Being with him is a help."

Jane laughed. "Are you kidding? He can't stand me. I'm driving him crazy."

"Come on," Emma said.

Jane's lipstick had rubbed off and was smudged around her mouth. "You tell me what he wants, Emma. You've known him forever."

"With a woman you mean?" Emma smiled vaguely. "I've never tried to figure out that part of Harry."

"Which is why he loves you so."

"Harry's an important friend to me."

"I know. He's wonderful at being friends. Brilliant at that."

"He means well, Jane."

"Does he?" Jane had a wilted, mooning look.

"He is with you after all. Why, do you think?" Emma said warmly.

"Perversity." Jane laughed. She pinched the bridge of her nose and shut her eyes. "Same reason I'm with him."

"Don't worry about it," Emma said. "You shouldn't."

Jane gazed at Emma's beautiful, placid face. No, one shouldn't worry about it. "I don't usually," she said, feeling a weight lift. "Probably *that* should worry me." Both women laughed. To this laughter, Harry Loder returned to the table, looking grateful.

It was still raining. They snapped Emma into a cab. She was off to see the van Gogh. "It's wonderful," Jane said. "It broke my heart."

"We'll see you tonight," Harry said, waving.

Jane watched the red lights swim off. "She's great," Jane said.

"She is," Harry said. "But she knows nothing about other people."

Jane crumpled a little. Harry grabbed her arm and strode them briskly off.

"What?" Jane said.

They stopped. "Aren't you coming back with me?" Harry looked down at her. She looked down at her shoes.

"I was going to help with the flowers for the opening, but . . ."

"Well?"

"Okay," she said brightly. She gazed forward with relief. "But will we ever find a cab?"

The sound of traffic swished down Park. Jane spotted one free cab heading uptown and dashed across the street but too late. She stayed on the opposite side. Across from her, Harry held his arm raised fixedly.

A cab stopped in front of him. He waved over the hood and ducked out of sight. Jane's heart leapt and she started to go to him. A car honked, swerved, sending her back to the curb, chuckling a little. When the light changed she crossed.

He'd left the door open and was over next to the window, looking out. "God," she said breathlessly, her eyes shining, "I nearly got run over." She fussed with her umbrella, collapsing it, and dropped a glove. "Whoops." She giggled and bent down for the glove. It had fallen in a puddle.

"What are you doing?" Harry's voice was annoyed. He did not look over. "Will you come on, Rachel? Just get in."

Jane stood up slowly, gazing at him through the open door. A strange sort of electric current ran through her. Harry's profile remained set, looking out his window. There was some worrying to do after all.

The Break-up

It was late when the phone rang in the distant reaches of the loft far from where the couple lay in bed. Through a row of open windows came the noises of Friday night — static on radios, the strained barking of dogs, someone drumming relentlessly on a garbage can top with a salsa beat.

"Forget it," a man's voice said.

"Owen." The woman beside him sat up wearily. But once off the bed she flew across the floor, her bare back flashing in and out of the grey light. She disappeared in the darkness and after a few moments emerged, walking purposefully, her black hair banging in a flap against her cheek. "It was Tim," she said, stopping at the dividing wall in a slash of murky light. "He's coming over."

"Christ, Liz."

"Honey, poor guy."

"Poor guy, my ass. I had lunch with him today and he was fine."

"Maybe it's finally hitting him."

"Doubt it," said Owen. The bed creaked and his dark figure moved off it. "Tim's not like that."

"Well, he is your best friend," Liz said.

"Not that I was asleep anyway." Owen found some shorts and strolled out into the larger room. He was a tall fellow in his late twenties. He opened the icebox and light fell on his pale eyes and mild, dreamy face.

"It's too hot to sleep," Liz said. "Too hot and too loud." Out the back window were the backs of other buildings, their windows pink, blue or yellow, covered with grates. "I don't know how you've stood it this long. And it's only July. What's going to happen in August?"

Lately Liz had been wondering a lot about what was going to happen in the future. She and Owen had been together now for eight months.

"We need beer," Owen said, coming back for a shirt. He took what was on top of the pile on a chair. Liz was fidgeting through her neat stacks of clothes on the wide windowsill, grumbling about something, probably that she didn't have what she wanted, a problem she had carrying things back and forth in paper bags from her tiny studio.

"You going?" Liz called from behind the divider.

Owen opened the door. Sometimes he felt that Liz was monitoring his every move.

"He sounded pretty bad on the phone," she shouted. "Kind of smashed."

Owen smiled. Good old Tim.

"He walked all the way from Ninety-ninth Street," Liz whispered, meeting Owen at the door. Behind her Tim's familiar figure was bent over a low table, swaying slightly, one shirttail untucked, his dark skin showing through with sweat. Tim looked as fit as always.

"Energetic of you," Owen said.

"I stopped in a few bars on the way," Tim said without enthusiasm. He picked up a magazine, looked at the cover, dropped it. "I hope you two lovebirds weren't asleep."

"Are you kidding?" Liz flopped on the couch, holding her arms out in the heat.

Owen offered beers. Liz shook her head. "So how was work?" Owen said, stretching out his legs.

Tim stared at the floorboards, elbows hard on his knees. "Couldn't do shit today." Some glass shattered outside, then there was laughter. "Shitty day," Tim said. More glass shattering. "But you know the thing that gets me? That it was just out of the middle of nowhere."

"It was pretty sudden," Owen said.

Tim's face lit up. "It was, wasn't it?"

Owen sipped his beer, keeping one eye on Tim.

75

Liz leaned forward, a pillow in her lap. "But you guys had been having problems, hadn't you? I mean, things weren't perfect."

"Of course they weren't perfect. Nothing's perfect. But they weren't that bad either."

"Well but Sonia must have thought so," Liz said tentatively.

"Sonia doesn't know what she thinks," Tim said.

"Oh," said Liz.

"I'm sorry, you just don't do this to people."

"I'm sure Sonia didn't want to," Liz said. "I'm sure she probably —"

"So what are you defending her for?"

"I'm not defending her. I'm just . . ." Liz glanced at Owen. He was reading the newspaper lying beside him.

"Hey," Owen said, not looking up. "Guess what's on."

"Owen," Liz said.

"Oh — sorry." Owen pushed the paper to the floor.

"She might have had a little more patience," Tim said, taking no notice of them. "Don't you think she could have had a little more patience?"

No one had an answer for that.

"Who wants another beer?" Owen smoothed his thighs and stood up.

"Actually maybe I will," Liz said.

Owen brought back a beer for Tim, who took it automatically. Owen had handed Tim hundreds of beers. It was a reassuring, familiar thing.

"She came and took the rest of her things this afternoon," Tim said. "It all looks totally different."

"She took a lot?" Owen said. This seemed typical of Sonia, something they both understood.

"No," Tim said vaguely. "Most of it was mine."

"I guess you haven't talked to her," Liz said.

Tim looked annoyed. "She just sends me bills and things, with no note, nothing."

"Yah," Liz said. "I know."

"It's ridiculous. Everything reminds me of the bitch."

"Have you thought about moving?" Liz said. She was trying to keep him talking. One of her theories was that people should talk all the time.

"Some of us don't have trust funds to dip into." Tim didn't look at Owen when he said this. "But the thing about Sonia," he went on bitterly, "was she had to get everyone to fall in love with her. Didn't matter who. The guy sitting next to her at a dinner party. She was very good at it. It was probably the one thing she knew how to do."

"I feel left out," Owen said. "She never tried it with me."

"You're not her type," Tim said. "You're too — I don't know — not her type." He turned back to Liz. "And so now this French guy."

"What French guy?" Owen said.

"Some fucking frog. Who the hell is he anyway? Knowing Sonia, she was probably seeing him before."

77

"She was not," Liz said.

"How do you know? What about James Peploe?"

"Oh that. That was before you guys were even together."

"James Peploe?" Owen said.

Liz nodded pityingly. If he paid more attention he'd know these things.

"God," Owen said in a hushed tone. "That guy really gets around."

"Wait a minute." Tim turned to Liz with new interest. "You knew the guy too."

Liz began twisting her hair into a bun. "Hardly," she said.

"That's not what I heard." Tim laughed.

Liz let her bun unravel like a coil. She looked at Tim, not amused. "He used to do stills, maybe twice for us. I'm sure he wouldn't even remember who I am."

"In that slinky little bathrobe?" Tim said. "I wouldn't be so sure."

"This is hardly a slinky bathrobe," Liz said but she was smiling, a blush spread across her throat.

"Owen, if I were you, I wouldn't let my girlfriend go around in such a slinky bathrobe."

Owen brightened. This was more like the old Tim. "She's hardly walking down Avenue B in it," he said.

"Maybe she should," Tim said in a strange, menacing tone. Liz plucked at her sleeve saying it really was a wreck and Owen laughed at least she was

78

wearing *something,* usually she was stark — when suddenly all their mutterings were drowned out by an earsplitting blast of music, a radio passing in a car down on the street. It was more like an explosion, deafening. The floor throbbed. Liz put her hands over her ears.

There was a blur where Tim had been and his back turned on them. The music trailed off, almost jaunty. They heard him mutter, "I can't stand it." His fist flew up and smacked his face. "I fucking loved her," he said between clenched teeth. The fist came up again.

Owen stood up. Liz looked at him desperately. "We know you did," Owen said. His hand went out. "We know you did."

"No!" Tim cried, wheeling around. "You don't." His eyes were brimming. "You just can't do this to people!" His gaze, shining fiercely, took in some unfathomable horror then grew dreamy, hypnotic. "I was going to ask her to marry me," he said.

"You were?" Owen whispered.

"Did Sonia know that?" Liz said, calculating.

Tim watched everything drift up into one corner of the loft and hover there. Then he snapped out of it. "She does now," he said. "But so what? So fuck her." He began to pace, stopped near the wall. "Hey, when are we going to go up here?" He was looking at a snapshot very closely, his voice booming. "Hook us a few tasty ones?"

"Soon," said Owen, picking up bottles. "We should."

"Why not this weekend?" Tim said with extra spirit, wiping his eyes.

"Can't," Owen said. "I've got to finish this story." He hoisted the trash bag out of its cardboard box, clinking the bottles inside. He'd lived there a year but still hadn't gotten around to buying a proper trash can. "Liz, this stinks," he said.

"Hey, I'm out of here," Tim said, slapping Owen on the back.

Liz saw them to the door. "Will you find a cab?" she said, hugging herself.

Tim touched her cheek. "So concerned," he said. "Such a concerned girl. Oh sorry," he added face-tiously. "I mean *woman*." Then his eyes went hard and blank and he turned away.

They stomped down the stairs, their voices echoing in the cement. "Really," Tim said, "a little fishing with the boys? Get Hal, just the guys . . ."

When Owen got back, Liz was wiping up in the kitchen. "Do you think he'll be all right?" she said.

Owen walked past her and began to shut the windows. "He's not going to commit suicide if that's what you mean." He snapped off the lights and headed for the bedroom.

"Owen." Liz followed him in the dark.

"You know what he just told me?" Owen gave a dry, bitter laugh. "He's going to try getting her back."

"You're kidding."

The bedroom was crisscrossed with grey light. Owen lay himself carefully down on the bed as if his bones were sore. With the windows shut it was quieter. "He also told me to watch out with you."

"He did?" Liz got into bed and gathered the sheet up around them, laying herself alongside him. "What do you think he meant by that?"

The Swan
in the Garden

"HE SEEMS NICE," said Mrs. Godwin, stirring her coffee with a small golden spoon. Through the rain-spattered window she could make out two figures in overcoats growing smaller on the wet, flattened grass. It was a grey day outside and everything seemed bruised. Inside a fire was going. Her husband and son were slumped on flowered sofas going through the Sunday papers. "Do you think, Bob?"

Both men were named Bob but only one of them, in his twenties, looked up. "He's okay," said Bob, looking into the fire. Having gotten a ride that morning from the city with his cousin Evelyn and her boyfriend, Albert, he knew more than he usually might have. Bob grinned to himself. "For a public defender." As a law student, this struck him as being particularly funny.

"Well Evie seemed happy," said Mrs. Godwin, sipping her coffee and continuing to muse out the window. The couple turned between a split rail fence and dipped out of sight. Mrs. Godwin had been keeping an eye on Evelyn ever since her sister, Evelyn's mother, had abandoned her family and run off to Barcelona with an art dealer.

"We're the first relatives he's met," Bob said. "He didn't look too relaxed."

Mrs. Godwin frowned. "They've been seeing each other how long?"

"Beats me," said Bob. "About a year."

"I know things are different today." Mrs. Godwin shook her head. "But I still don't understand it."

Bob turned the pages of the newspaper, not reading. "Who does?" he smirked.

On the other side of the woods beyond the field was an empty parking lot and a boarded-up shack. Evelyn and Albert emerged arm-in-arm from some dripping trees. An avenue of oaks curved up to a mansion in the Charles II style. The gardens were closed for the season.

"It's usually much nicer than this," said Evelyn cheerfully. She had been looking forward to showing Albert the gardens. Usually it was Albert who did the showing, taking her to meet his friends, explaining to her about his cases. But Albert Nastro did not look happy. "Are you sure you feel like walking?" she said.

Albert regarded her from beneath a dark brow. "I'm here, aren't I?" It had taken him a long time to agree to come out to meet the Godwins at all.

The December mist hung around them, hung over the lawns which were clipped and brown like a doormat. Evelyn led him to a map of the gardens, a board mounted on poles, to show him where they were. Albert went strolling by, preferring to see for himself. He headed for the first white arrow. It was his way to follow directions and complain about them — the same attitude he had towards the law and his job — critical and cantankerous.

Evelyn took a deep breath. She was often taking deep breaths lately. Her roommate, Lavinia Presten, was getting married and Evelyn would have to move out. Albert had not suggested that she move in with him all the way. She lived with him mostly already. He liked her to have a place of her own, just in case.

They had the garden to themselves. Fog hovered like a lid over one of the ponds. A statue shrouded in canvas was tied at the ankles with rope. She wanted to tell him that underneath was Diana with breast bared but he was a shadow now, weaving through a colonnade.

In the summer the gardens were ruffled with flowers. On tranquil evenings limousines would spill out wedding parties onto the driveway. A distracted bride furling her train, bridesmaids teetering on high heels. They would line up in front of an exploded rhododendron bush to have their picture taken. It was something other people did, got married. She and Albert had a different thing between them. When they first met, their understanding of each other was so complete, marriage was beside the point.

She caught up with him under the shriveled arborway of the Primrose Path. As they wandered through the rose bushes wrapped with burlap and twine in the sunken Rose Garden, Evelyn asked him if anything was the matter.

He eyed her suspiciously. It was Sunday. They usually had some kind of a fight on Sunday. He mumbled something about work and moved stiffly down the steps of the Italian Gardens. Evelyn always felt something enchanted inside the walls, probably from a favorite children's book. The atmosphere was lost on Albert. At the far end, under a green pavilion, they stood staring into a goldfish pond clogged with leaves.

"Albert," she said, "what's going to become of us?"

He glanced at her in terror. "How should I know?"

"Yes, but what do you think?"

"Evelyn," he said, suffering.

"It's just a question."

"I think," he said, "that everything is fine."

They left the garden under a brick arch and turned down a narrow path dark with hedges. "But the future?" She could hear the tiresome tone in her voice. Once their understanding had extended to the future, they had agreed the future was a trap.

Albert's interest was taken up by the thatched-roof playhouse at the end of the tunnel. Through the windows was a tea party for the dolls, sitting stiffly on pillows, with legs extended. Back in the shadows were more toys and the dim outline of a rocking horse. "Spoiled brats," said Albert. He'd grown up in a small house in Billerica with four brothers, playing street hockey during the slushy spring thaws, watching the Boston Bruins on TV.

They crossed a wet lawn, passing the mansion. "But do you have some vision of the future?" Evelyn said.

"Ev, I'm twenty-seven. Give me a break." He inspected the busts set into the niches in the wall. "Hey, who are these guys?" he said brightly.

"Don't know," said Evelyn, shrugging. She slouched across the lawn. Above her, a stone satyr kicked a gleeful foot into the air. She went around the tarp-covered pool onto the gravel path leading around the pond.

"Hey." Albert caught up with her. "Aren't you happy with the way things are?"

She turned to him gratefully. "I just need to know what's going on sometimes. I want to know what you think."

"I don't think anything," he said.

Her face fell. "But you must —"

"Evelyn, do you think other people sit around and talk about this all the time?"

"What other people?"

His arm flew up. "I don't know. That's not the point." He gazed off, exasperated. He saw some swans gliding on the glassy water. "My brother, for instance."

Evelyn rolled her eyes. Mark again.

"Yeah. Do you think Mark and Katya sit around and discuss their relationship every other second?"

"Every other second?"

"Okay, at all."

"I don't know, Albert."

He nodded, a gesture he used in court having made a point. He set off with a jaunty stride. Some swans had landed and were waddling towards them. One graceful head floated at the end of a long neck. Evelyn felt soothed by the beautiful thing. Its beak opened, showing an obscene pink tongue. It hissed, startling her.

Albert chuckled, not surprised. "They're vicious little devils," he said and marched on.

A ghostly pagoda with white pillars appeared among the bare trees. Albert inspected the filigree dome. "The Temple of Love," said Evelyn in a grim tone.

"Listen," said Albert. "I work my ass off all week long. I have everyone at me. Can't I have one day when you're not at me too?"

Evelyn looked down at her boot and toed the mud. "I don't mean to be at you," she said.

"Well you are."

She watched him stomp off over the Japanese bridge. When they'd first met, Evelyn had felt a serene unfolding. Life had seemed to open and open. It was a wonderful thing. She reminded herself of that now. She reminded herself that he loved her. It just wasn't his way to show it.

"I'm sorry I don't give you peace and quiet," she said. "That's a terrible thing." He nodded, still mad. "It's just that I need to know if —"

Albert wheeled around, his shoulders swollen, and exploded. "For Christ sake, Evelyn, can't you leave it alone? What do you want me to say? That I'm not sure? Is that what you're waiting for me to say?"

"What?" she whispered.

His head twitched with anger.

"About us?" she said. "About me?"

He dropped his hands. "You push too hard." His voice was almost a whine. "Why can't you just leave things alone? Do you need to know everything?"

"I should this," she said.

He stared up at the dark trees. "I can't help it," he said.

"I didn't know . . ." She brushed by him. Tree roots erupted out of the pine-needled earth.

"Awww," he said in a lighter tone. "Can't you be patient?"

"You mean wait?" She stopped and turned around.

He looked fearful. "No, I mean, do what you have to do."

She was filled with confusion. "Then . . . if . . ." but her thoughts would not settle. They walked on.

At the shell mosaics of the wall fountain, Albert stopped her. "Just try to understand my position," he said. They were facing the scalloped niche and his voice echoed strangely. It seemed to be a voice Evelyn had never heard before. His arm came up around her, squeezing her stiffly. It was a foreign arm.

"I am," she said. Her mind was racing. She'd been too certain. One could never know another person's mind. She'd been so wrong . . . and with Albert. The possibilities for misunderstanding seemed to multiply before her eyes, a hundred hills overlapping in the distance, chaotic and out of control.

Albert went bounding up the terrace steps, two at a time, away from her. She called to him, "It's only because I —" She began to say *love* but the word didn't come. It had been frightened off. "I care," she said.

"Care a little less," he said over his shoulder.

On the upper terrace were Sphinx statues, marble faces staring across the lawn, their expressions placid and knowing, the ribbons lifting their hair.

Evelyn stood at the balustrade with her hands on the wet stone and stared down the vista. There were two rows of dark green hedges running parallel, tapering away from her into a grey mist. She could just make out an iron gate but could not tell where the garden ended and the world beyond began.

His footsteps were going away from her. "Albert," she called. He turned around. He took a deep breath. His eyes were closed. "Can we please stop talking about this now?" he said.

She did stop and inside her something stopped too.

The Feather in
the Toque

THEY WOKE EARLY, a still morning, all the summer stores closed, all the summer renters gone back to the city. It felt as if they were the last people left on the island.

It was grey out, the clouds low, the sky the same color as the light grey of the bedroom. It had been a gentle night and there was tranquility in the room. No cars hummed by on the out-of-the-way lane. The neighbor was not, for a change, riding his lawnmower. Outside the leaves had started to curl and some had started to fall.

The man got up and strolled naked into the hall. He lifted a shade, continued along the passageway to his study.

The woman lay in bed. She was younger than

the man and in these few months had glimpsed a different way of living. Yesterday they'd had lunch with some friends of the man. How was Sabine? someone asked about one of his old girlfriends. The man shook his head as if the news were sad. Number two on the way, he said and slurped at an oyster shell. The woman thought of this lying in bed. Number two on the way. He'd said it with a hostile tone. Through the window she could see a white sun sparkling on the backwater. She got up to run a bath.

The bathroom was at the corner of the house with windows facing in two directions. The faucet screeched through the pipes, water splashed in the old tub, echoing in the bare wainscoted room.

Suddenly a dark thing skimmed across the ceiling. The woman followed it into the bedroom, calling the man. A small bird was flapping up in a corner. The man appeared in the doorway.

"Look," the woman said. "We've got to get it out." Immediately she realized this was a useless thing to say. She folded her arms over her bare chest and ignored the man's sidelong glance. It was sure to be annoyed.

The bird alit on the ceiling fan. Its head ticked from side to side like a cuckoo then it broke into a frantic flurry again. It veered crazily. It hit the wall. "Oh. I hate that," the woman said.

The man lifted the window sashes all the way. He left the windows open at least partway all summer long whether he was in the house or not. He went on a lot of trips.

The bird flew into the bathroom. The woman watched intently, willing the bird to find its way out. It swooped back over their heads.

"Does this happen much?" the woman said.

The man was putting on his bathrobe. "It will fly out," he said, unconcerned. He was a tall man and had to bend down to peer out the window. He grew interested in something over by the toolshed. His hand toyed in the large pocket of his bathrobe, planning something.

The woman stood on her tiptoes to look at the bird. It was a sparrow. The soft breast was panting, its tiny heart as hard as a peppercorn inside. It was disconcerting for her, but exhilarating too, this wild beating thing. Behind her the man walked out.

She remembered her bath and went to shut it off. The water was up to the brim, all the hot would be gone. The sound of wings flapping was eerie in the sudden quiet. The man's footsteps could be heard going down the stairs.

The whole ground floor was an open room with the kitchen around to the side. Past where the man was walking there was a bookshelf. Earlier in the summer, alone in the house, the woman had been looking for a book and had come across a framed snapshot behind a stack of paperbacks. It wasn't hidden, but it wasn't out either. The picture was of a woman in leopard pants with a toque set jauntily on her head. A shiny feather curled around the toque, shooting chicly off to one side. The woman slipped the photograph back behind the books. She did not mention it to the man. They had only just met, it was none of her business. In fact, it had given her kind of a kick to find it.

She thought of the picture now, downstairs where the man was. She did not like the feeling.

The dark blur ducked into the bathroom. The woman shut the door. She stood on the cold floor, waiting. "Come on," she said and felt foolish.

Wings smacked the walls, the woman looked up. Just then the bird dipped down and shot out one window, undulating in a path directly away from her and the house. She almost cried out but something stopped her. No one would hear.

She lifted the drain and water trickled down through the whole house. The first time she'd been in the house no one was there and all the doors had been open. The air blew in, everything was breezy. Books lay about, newspapers rustled on the table. Someone had been making tomato sandwiches. There was a wonderful feeling of light in the room. The people who had been in it must have been as languid and bright.

She stepped into the lukewarm tub. Out the window was a view of the lawn, the bench where no one ever sat, the grand round tree in the center, its leaves going orange in spots and red.

Up to her neck in it, she found the water cooler than she'd thought. Still it was warmer than the air. She wouldn't move yet. She listened downstairs for some sounds of the man beneath her. He could be inside or out. No doors had banged but that didn't mean anything. The doors were always wide open.

She stood up and reached for a towel. Standing in the raised tub she noticed a woman's comb on one of the high bare shelves. She felt a pang and went to examine it. It was a tortoiseshell comb. On crowded city streets one might catch sight of a stranger's reflection in a store window and with a start recognize the stranger as oneself. This happened to the woman. Holding the comb she saw it was hers.

It gave her a kind of thrill to find something of hers in the man's house. But it surprised her too. The man would never have noticed. That sort of thing did not matter to him. She put it back on the shelf, leaving something of hers for the next woman to find.

THREE

The Knot

I

"Will we ever fight?"

She smiled, nestled in his arm. "No. I mean, a little. But not really."

"It's hard to imagine," he said. She nodded. "In fact, I can't really see it." She shook her head, agreeing.

They were facing out the window, watching the kids playing football in the parking lot across the street. Dark footprints showed on the snow, making spirals.

"That's for other people," he said and took a deep breath and put both arms around her.

"And we're not like other people?" she said. He shook his head, and they laughed.

II

"Do we have to talk about this now?"

They were lying in bed, staring at the ceiling, not touching each other.

"When else will we?" she said.

"Sweetheart, I'm exhausted. Can't we talk about it tomorrow?"

She didn't answer.

He breathed heavily out of his nose. "Come on. Give me a break."

"Okay, goodnight," she said.

They lay in silence.

"We will," he said. His voice grew faint. "We'll talk about it tomorrow."

"Sure," she said to herself.

"We will."

"You always say that," she said.

"Please," he groaned. "I can't stand this. I need some sleep."

"So do I," she said. "We both do."

"Then let's stop torturing each other. It's ridiculous."

"It is ridiculous," she said, turning on her side, away from him. "You're right."

III

In the fall, they met over soup.

"You look good," she said. "Thinner."

"I'm okay," he said, annoyed.

"Really?"

"Sure." He pushed his bowl away. "I have a job I hate. No one wants to buy my screenplays. And the woman I was living with wakes up one morning and decides to move out. I'm great. Couldn't be better."

"Please," she said, her glance flitting about the table. "Pete."

"What do you expect me to say?"

"I don't know. I just hoped —"

"What? That I'd be nice? Were you nice to me?"

"I guess not," she whispered.

He took a deep breath. "Listen, Cyn, I'm sorry. I guess I still can't see you. I don't understand what happened. One minute you were there and everything was fine and suddenly you ditched out on me."

"Everything was not fine."

"Okay. But you still ditched out on me."

"Do you want us to go over —?"

"No," he said. Around them at other tables people were having pleasant, chatty lunches. He was shaking his head. "I still don't get it though."

"We weren't talking," Cynthia said.

"And we can't start again? You expect too much, you need too much attention."

"But . . ."

"You do," he said. "I don't know why you think you're different from everyone else." He looked down at the soup in front of him, the awful soup.

"I tried, Pete."

He began to eat his soup. "If you think that, you'll never be happy. That's not trying. I think you want to have an unhappy life."

She looked off. Out the window people were hurrying by in the bright cold day, busy, with a purpose. "I don't," she said.

"You're a very spoiled girl," he said. He put down his spoon. "I can't eat this shit."

"No," she said. "Neither could I."

IV

"Peter?" He looked up at a bicycle coming toward him.

"Cynthia," he said, walking over to the curb.

"Hi," Cynthia said and put her feet down, still sitting on the bicycle seat. "I thought that was you."

"What are you doing down here?"

"Subletting for the summer. How are you?"

He frowned at her. "Fine. I'm fine. How're you?"

"Good. Hot though." She laughed. "Can you believe this heat?"

"I know, it's bad," he said. "I finally got an air conditioner."

"Did you? Good for you."

He nodded. "It makes a difference."

"I'll bet." She glanced over his shoulder at a woman walking a dog. The dog rounded its back and crouched on its hind legs. "So how is everything?" she said. "I hear you sold a script."

"Yup. They bought *Cowgirls,* and gave me a three-picture deal."

"That's great. Congratulations."

"Thanks." He stared at her. "Believe it or not, it actually looks like they'll make it."

"Really? Are they shooting anytime . . . ?"

"Next month actually. They've got Connie Carver for it."

"Connie Carver. You really have hit the big time."

"I get to visit the set in Montana."

"Fun. I'm stuck here all summer."

"Still at the museum?"

She shrugged, smiled. "Still am."

He nodded, not smiling.

"So, have you —" she began. "Are you seeing anyone?"

"Actually, I'm seeing Laura again."

"Are you? God. So that's good?"

"It is," he said.

"That's good," she said.

They both looked off down the street. Some

smoke was billowing out of a black tube near some sawhorses and a black hole in the road. "You?" he said.

She nodded.

"Nice guy?"

"So far so good," she said. "We'll see."

He took a breath. "Listen, I gotta get going."

"Oh me too." She put her foot on a pedal.

"It was nice seeing you, Cynthia," he said. He reached up to her face and she drew back, startled. "You have something . . ." he said.

She understood and moved forward. "What?" she said, smiling nervously.

He brushed her chin. "Just a — I don't know — little . . ."

The touch was like a charge. Something rose up between them and bound them there. The awkwardness was not gone, but for a moment, they could not move. They stared into each other's eyes, fascinated by what they saw.

A Thrilling Life

FRANK MANAGER KNEW how to make a girl sparkle, he knew the right things to say. If a day went
by without his managing to flirt at least once, he
would fall into a little depression. He was always
flirting shamelessly with receptionists, waitresses,
ticket tellers, making them blush. His eyes bore
into them, an Indian look with strange seriousness,
while his mouth flashed a smile. He flirted whether
he was on his own or not. He seemed to prefer to
flirt when he was in a woman's company, especially
if she happened to be his girlfriend.

Frank had a lot of different girlfriends. He got
bored easily and didn't hold on to anyone for long.
The girl who was with him the longest had just
hung around for a couple of years. She was sort of

out of it. You had to be sort of out of it to be with Frank.

Frank was not a candidate for the long run. He might just as well have been wearing a banner which said FRIVOLITY. He had supreme confidence and an inviolate manner. It was just what I was looking for.

I had just gotten out of a bad thing and the guy I'd left was in pretty miserable shape. I was tired of being with people in miserable shape and of feeling that I was part of the reason for it. Frank, I could see, was not your vulnerable type. I suppose things didn't matter enough to hurt him. And Frank couldn't hurt me. My heart was already broken.

We were never introduced. Frank just came brashly up to me, the only single woman he didn't know. We were on a porch, drinking, friends of his, friends of mine. The summer evening had begun to wilt, the flat water gone pale and white. He sat beside me on the steps and made fun of the shoes I was wearing. I was not used to being teased and I tried to tease back but was not very good at it. He smiled but I could see it wasn't working too well. I thought, this man could teach me a thing or two.

He'd been around. Sprinkled through his conversation — he appeared a lot the next few days — were references to villas in Spain, hippie girlfriends, trips to Alaska, silk from Thailand. He had theories about the Shining Path in Peru and ways to cook peacock. He was backing a restaurant on the Thames. At one point I asked him an inane question, something about what his father did, and Frank flashed me an annoyed eye. The look was involuntary and he tried to cover it up but it had shown through. There was rage beneath the banter and charm. I was intrigued.

We began to see each other. Frank liked things that moved quickly, dramatic weather, wide views. The man I'd recently left had never really decided how much, if at all, he believed in love.

Frank drove me home one night. We sat in the front seat of his car, a windy night in the city. For some reason the streetlights were out on my block and everything was black. You don't have to go, he said. I told him I did. He kissed me. We stayed there, skirting the gearshift, for a while. Finally I got out. I was dizzy. I went around to his window to say goodnight and his arm reached out, drawing me close. Kiss me, he said, his white teeth showing in the darkness. Give me the best possible kiss ever. The kiss that makes you fall in love, the kiss that you would give to someone so that he would fall in love forever.

What did he mean? I tried to see his eyes in the dark but they looked flat, like flat spots of ink. I had a lot to learn. This sort of flirtation was new to me.

The magazine I worked for had a strong left-wing bent. There were always raging political discussions going on, the office itself a raging, disorganized mess. If the subject of sex came up it was usually attached to a political figure or part of local gossip. All day I was surrounded by earnest men with furrowed brows who read Balzac in the mailroom. The more jovial ones delivered double entendres with a wry, jaded air, not coming out from behind their desks. Sex was something other people did. Sometimes the writers swept in with an exotic air, smelling faintly of alcohol, flushed and distracted. If they noticed you the first time, they would forget the next time they came in.

I don't know what goes on in a man's brain and I certainly didn't know what went on in Frank's. He was like a little boy, thinking happily of himself, going after things. He had worked as a designer, he'd been in television, he'd done God knows what and now, as far as I could tell, was investing here and there, starting little companies. He traveled a lot. He told me he wanted a thrilling life. I had no idea what a thrilling life entailed, but I could imagine a lot of things. I wanted a thrilling life too.

Frank and I did not keep track of each other. When we came together it was pleasant and happy, as long as he was entertained. If Frank wasn't being sufficiently entertained, a dead look would pass over his face and the whole room would feel it. But as soon as he snapped out of it, he was lively again. I met lots of people with Frank. He took me around. Back from a trip, he'd have amusing sto-

ries to tell me. When he was gone, I returned to
my usual routine — double bills at the Regency,
using the stray invitations which floated through
the office — parties or openings or screenings.

Frank was in another world — weekends in Eu-
rope, glamorous friends. I was not a part of it but
it was interesting to me. I paid close attention to
him, to see how people behaved in that world.
Frank was always pleasant, always polite. He was
polite the way a waiter is polite, gracious, never too
personal. So there were no screaming fights, no
terrible dragging hours of silence and fury. It was
all very laissez-faire. People at the office mentioned
how well I looked.

But Frank did not seem to feel as if he belonged
anywhere. He was always rushing off, rushing
away. Or he glanced over your shoulder to something better going on over there, someplace he'd
rather be. In a restaurant, Frank's gaze flew up
suddenly, expecting someone else to arrive. Then,
returned to himself, he would notice me again, and
ask me if I wanted another drink.

After a certain point, my friends spoke up. He
doesn't care about you, they said. Most of them
hadn't even met Frank. I let go of some of my
friends. I was sick to death of the closed life I'd
been leading and Frank had put me in high spirits.
Male friends were especially appalled. What do you
see in this guy? they said. He's a lizard. You women
are so stupid.

What they didn't see was how Frank could sweep you away. Such brashness can be intoxicating. If someone offers you such a lift, why pass it up?

Frank had a certain way of touching. When he made contact, he seemed to drift into a dream. His whole body tilted forward, his eyes closed, and he seemed to concentrate the way a cloud might concentrate, loose and weightless, and the way his hands moved was like clouds too, hardly touching the skin. He seemed to be listening to a sound far away. But he was, for a little while, happy with where he happened to be.

One evening after a nap, Frank made soup. He set our plates down at opposite ends of the table. It was a test. He sat over his steaming bowl all the way down the long table and smiled at me. I smiled back, made a comment about his childhood and didn't say anything more. When Frank got that way, I ignored it.

It was harder to ignore the girls. Frank's old girlfriends were all over the place. They were everywhere I went.

A woman wearing clanging bracelets nudged me during a chaotic dinner party. "We're Eskimo sisters," she said through dark lips. She had known Frank way back, before all the money. Frank used to be shy, she said, even with girls, she laughed, if you can believe it.

A different time I overheard a Southern woman saying men like Frank Manager were a dime a dozen. "I ought to know," she drawled. "I've known 'em all."

A clean-cut girl with combed hair and pearl earrings cornered me at a Christmas party. "Do you think Frank Manager is as weird as I did?" she said with a penetrating look. Suddenly I got very protective of Frank. I don't know why. He was not, you might say, protective of me.

"So you're Frank's friend," said the hostess and introduced me around the room with an ironic smile. I thought I detected a number of eyebrow-knowing female eyes.

What was I doing with someone like Frank? I knew better. A lot of Frank's girls didn't, but I did. I was mesmerized by something. I think it had a lot to do with the fact that I was there at all. I had a perverse impulse to see if I could handle it.

"You're not jealous, are you?" said Frank on the way home in a cab. We'd spent all evening in a dark, glittering room. "You don't seem like the jealous type."

"No," I said. His arm was around me and I was happy to be with him alone. He seemed content and I was glad to be a part of his contentment. It had not thrilled me to watch some woman with a bow on her head perch herself breezily on Frank's knee most of the night. I ignored it. Slowly it fell away and I felt as if I were joining the ranks of those people adjusted to the world — the happier tribe which doesn't dwell on the lack of power one has or on those small, passing feelings. Emotions, I was beginning to see, were not a part of the thrilling life.

I heard things, I was warned. There were rumors about Frank — liaisons in other countries, shifty business deals. I asked him nothing. I was not going to listen to other people. So far he treated me fine. He was always perfectly civil to me, perfectly straightforward. If he was vague about his plans, it was, he explained, because he didn't want to answer to anyone. I liked that. I wanted that myself. Frank didn't ask for anything, so I was not obliged to him. It was the serious ones who hurt you — they watched too carefully, they were easily disappointed, they too quickly took offense. It was the close, loving ties that wreaked so much havoc. I was learning to keep things to myself. I was learning to be free.

Then something started to happen. With all this happy, free feeling, I felt something stir inside me — small muffled explosions, like a car backfiring into cotton: I was thinking of Frank. It was, of course, inappropriate to be thinking of Frank that way. I was aware of that. I was perfectly aware of the whole situation. I had it under control. Besides, it wasn't so bad, really, to feel again.

I didn't say anything, but I think Frank sensed something. When I turned a particularly bright face to him, his flat eyes warned me Don't, don't you dare. He made half-plans or didn't call. He showed up late or not at all. One night he told me straight out he did not want to be loved. It's not what I'm after, he said.

I thought somebody should have told Frank to stop doing those things that make people love you. I had gotten better at hiding things. I had learned from Frank. When Frank walked into a room, his expression said, "I've just come from the most marvelous world." It was a lie, of course, he didn't think that. But Frank was always a good liar.

One Sunday afternoon, pouring rain, we sat in some dive, shouldered against the bar by men with pool sticks. Frank looked tired and I asked him what was wrong. I wasn't feeling particularly vivacious myself. He told me he didn't think he could make me happy. I asked him why not. Because, he said, I cannot be constant in my affections. When he looked at me he might just as well have been looking down a long dim hall to a door closed at the end. Frank was getting tired of me. I hadn't expected it so soon. Constancy of affection? I thought. Who needed that?

One night Frank and I were lying in bed and he mentioned the name of a woman. Had I heard of her? No, I said, I hadn't. Well, said Frank in a chatty tone, she was a woman he'd been having an affair with for some time now. She lived outside Rome. She was coming to visit. He told me he would, of course, be seeing her. He didn't ask me if I'd mind. He simply gave me the information, patted me sympathetically on the arm and drew me closer. I might have said something then but I didn't. It was something to ignore. If I ignore it, I thought, it won't bother me. But that didn't work so well this time. I tried to reason it away. I had never really tried that before. It seemed like the adult thing to do. It took some concentration. I held very still. I thought of all the reasons it didn't matter. I thought about our being free. I thought, what good would it do to tell him something anyway? I felt very adult, reasoning away my emotions. I didn't say a thing. It was a peculiar feeling, it felt very strange. It was like being dead.

Now and then I hear about Frank. He's started a marble importing business with an old girlfriend. The woman with the bangles stays in his apartment when she's in town. Frank's girls are still all around. They've made the adjustment to see Frank in a certain way, as a friend. I don't seem to be able to make the change.

From what I gather, the new girl is a surprise. She's quiet, serious, self-contained. She doesn't seem like the type to badger him, something Frank will like. Though he won't like the silence. Silence makes Frank restless.

If I ever ran across her, I wouldn't try to tell her anything, try to give her advice. I tried it once. I had it tried on me. It doesn't work. And, really, why should it? Secretly each girl thinks she'll be a turning point. Who knows? Maybe she will be. Things change. One always hopes.

Still I have a certain sympathy for her, one she has no idea about. I understand what she's going through. I know the dreamy expression on her face. I know it from the inside out. I had it once myself.

Île Sèche

IN THE MORNING before sailing for Île Sèche, they went into town. The boathand dropped them off, then sped away to get ice.

The girl and the man strolled through the narrow streets, stepping aside to let the cars pass. Neither of them had been on St. Bart's before, but the man knew other islands and was pointing out charming aspects of the architecture. The man was tall, at least a foot taller than the girl, with grey hair and an eager pleasant expression, which suddenly vanished at the sound of a jackhammer down the road. The girl, following behind, looked the ingénue. She was an actress and that was her usual role. She was in the middle of asking a question when the man grabbed her out of the way of a car.

Meg Gillian flushed a little and walked on. How odd it was that they were here together. She did not know Charles Howe well, though she'd been hearing the name Charles Howe for years. It was not until her recent success off-Broadway that he'd swooped down on her from that lofty place where deals were made and plays produced. She was rather frightened but, mostly, flattered. People warned her to watch out. Flashing a smile, Charles Howe said they were right. She laughed at his teasing. Almost a year before, she'd been weeping in a bathtub, the only private place in the loft, because the fellow she was living with did not — not yet anyway — though he said he would, eventually — want to get married.

The man stopped at a motorbike shop. "Why don't you take one?" he said. "While I make my calls." Meg assumed the calls included the other girlfriend, an art director in California. Meg had not asked him about her.

A small traffic jam was forming. The jackhammer made a deafening noise. "So?" said the man. "Take a little spin?" He looked down at the girl.

She hesitated. They waited for someone to come over and help them.

"Do you or not?" he shouted above the noise. "Because if you don't . . ."

"Actually," she said and fingered the rubber grip of the handlebars.

"What?" he screamed.

She felt suddenly very far from everything. "I don't know," she said. "I don't think I trust myself on these."

"Well. Then. Then we shouldn't hang around. Better get a cup of coffee. Safer."

"They just make me nervous," she said, but that wasn't it. She'd ridden them before. It was something else.

He had already turned and was walking away. "Much safer. Yes, let's get a cup of coffee."

At the end of the street was a steep hill. "I think I'll keep going and walk up to the lighthouse," Meg said. They'd seen it from the boat, a white milk bottle with a red cap.

"Yes, you do that." He seemed relieved. He took her grocery bag, adding it to the one he carried. They set off apart.

Once away from him her step grew lighter and she practically ran up the hill. Up close the lighthouse was small. Down in the harbor she could see his boat, *Vapeur,* placid and certain, its bow pointing the same way as the bows of the other boats, but more lovely because it was his boat. At night his boat was like a cradle, the clouds ghostlike through the oval windows. The wind flapped the canvas.

That afternoon they anchored by the ribbed cliffs of Île Sèche. The boathand brought them ashore in the dinghy, declining the invitation to walk around the island with them. He wasn't one for climbing in high places, he said with a bright expression, and didn't like the look of those goats.

The beach where they landed was grey and white, the stones fist-size, like paperweights. They tied on their sneakers. Meg saw brain coral, with its maze pattern, and smooth rocks with smooth holes bored partway through, and bits that looked like petrified snowflakes. She reached for a goat bone that was like an ivory shoehorn and *splat!* near her hand, a yellow foamy crap from the sky landed on the smooth stones. A pelican, eerily close to her, angled by on crippled wings. Then she saw the man heading up the hill.

It rose steeply. The dots they'd seen from afar became cactus plants close up, swollen pincushions with tilted maroon chimneys and, in the dark red fur on top, one tiny shocking-pink flower clashing with the red velvet. The man and the girl crossed a wide bald place hammocked between two bluffs. The grass had been bitten away. Startled goats flashed brown rears before gamboling off on thin legs. From the boat the bluffs had seemed huge, a landscape in a Wyoming western. Up close they were small enough to climb. It was the reverse of how perspective was supposed to work, that things turned smaller when you drew close to them. It had happened before with the lighthouse.

They climbed the steep bluff. The volcanic rock, melted thousands of years ago, was hardened into palm-size steps, soft and sloping like melted wax. Charles Howe was behind her, a different climbing from the late nights in New York up deserted stairs.

They reached the top in a thick wind. It was lovely to stand there with the black rock dropping in folds beneath them. A band of goats on the next peak eyed them.

On the man's large face was a rapturous expression. One hand was clamped on his sun hat. The girl was breathless.

"This is all right, isn't it?" he said.

"It's beautiful." She was smiling.

"Look." Charles Howe dismissed the horizon with his hand. "Nothing between us and England."

It was like no place the girl had seen, this primitive island with the pelicans angling by on their prehistoric wings. A blue haze hung at the horizon in a fine misty net. Meg had spent time on other islands, stepping off rocky beaches in Maine into the dark pines, discovering things in the dark shadows. Something as small as a mushroom, its hat ruffled at a dapper angle, could become the most remarkable thing, rare, something to examine.

The man stepped along the razorback. Meg noticed shells cracked open by flying birds. To one side was a straight drop to the water pounding its head against the cliff.

"Wait," Meg said and was surprised at the weakness in her voice.

Charles Howe turned, frowning. "You all right?"

She nodded, stunned. There was nothing difficult about where they were walking, a sort of ledge. She'd walked narrow places hundreds of times, but the dark-shaded ocean was teeming straight down and his hardness threw her off. Her bearings suddenly went and her hand was suspended, toward him.

He grabbed her arm just as she tipped. He grabbed it hard and pulled her near and set her firmly again on her feet. Then he released her. She glanced desperately off. Neither spoke of it. It had hardly happened. Her heart was beating wildly.

The man set off, to be away from her. They went down the melted steps on the other side. The girl, feeling the bruise where he'd gripped her, felt light-headed and, catching her breath, calm. They stepped back on the ground, a crazed network of goat paths. She wanted to say something to him. "Look at the light," she said. The cactus plants were lit in fuzzy outlines, the tassel-ended grass flared in blond torches. Nothing moved.

"What?" said the man ahead of her. His voice was impatient again.

But she would not be scared. "Look," she repeated.

He turned around but did not look where she was pointing. He looked at her. His face was blank and inscrutable.

Still she refused to see it. She took in the sun.

The air was fresh and balmy, and across the flat ocean stretched a bright carpet to the sun, which was lower now and from this height made everything expansive and wide. She picked up a small stone and threw it near him, thinking it was what a playful, spirited girl would do. She was determined not to be defeated by him. And yet, something tightened in her chest.

They wandered apart, he drifting down, she staying higher along the ridge. There was no water on the island, only rain pooled in marshy valleys. No one could live on Île Sèche. It was barren and beautiful. The next bluff cast a dark blue shadow on the next hill. The goats hobbled over the volcanic rock, the cactus bristled. They too might skitter across the hillside, coming alive at night, growling in a low eerie way.

A white round thing bounced off some rocks and landed near the girl's feet. It was a seashell. In the almond-shaped opening was a red claw folding up. As she watched, the claw pulled itself in slowly, its joints ancient, creaking, furtive. You don't notice me, it seemed to say, you aren't seeing me at all. Nearby, tucked beneath a ledge, was another shell, smaller, then another beside that, all of them hiding their blue-edged fingers like reclusive old women drawing knuckles under shawls, tightening around a precious brooch. Some shells were chalk-white with turret ends. Others were turban shells, swirled black and pearl, tipped like a meringue.

The shells were everywhere, the plateau was covered with them.

She turned toward the bay where the boat was.
She could make out the boathand's figure on the
bow, slumped into a sailbag, reading or sleeping.
Down in the anchorage the boat looked small. The
little claws had climbed a long way.

Her heart choked at such a wonderful thing, she
was bursting with it. Again she found herself on a
high place with water below, something surging
within her, and nearby, the man, inescapable.
Where was he now? She looked around. There, she
saw the white sun hat at a distance down the slope.
He was sitting on a rock, facing the bay, watching
his boat.

"You should see it up here," she called to him.
"It's covered with hermit crabs!" Her voice sailed
through the quiet air, thin and clear. He was not
that far away, he could hear. There was nothing
between them, no trees, no wind, no bird sounds.
The rumble of the surf was somewhere, but far off,
part of another watery world, down by the cliffs,
far away.

But the man was not a part of any world. He did
not turn around.

The girl had not believed before what his teasing
voice had said. Now she understood it in another
way, with his back to her, his white hat obtuse and
silent. She could go ahead and exclaim over the

light, be a part of this open air, take in the sea, walk the uneven surface of this hillside with its loose rocks and cactus tubes and hermit crabs, but she should realize what part he was playing in it — his own. He had brought her here, it was his boat, they could puzzle out the constellations together, but that was all. He was, said Charles Howe's back to her, separate. He would not be a part of her.

She walked, quickly.

Maybe this was the better way to be. Certainly it had not worked with the fellow before, melting into each other's lives, then being miserable with the blurring. Something *should* be different. There was something about this man, that when she was in his arms they were always warm and long and she was protected in them. It silenced her. He stroked her gently, his profile staring off in the dark, and close to him, she could admire his stubbornness, that he would not put up with ridiculous things.

And there were many ridiculous things. She had become one of them.

She walked faster, stumbled, increased her pace.

They returned to the anchorage of Gustavia. The man had guests flying in the next day.

In the evening the man and the boathand went into town to buy supplies and the girl took a swim in the harbor. The sun, orange and low on the horizon, popped out of sight, turning the sky pink-violet. Clouds rose up, golden, fisted, dwarfing the islands. In the dim light the rocks guarding the harbor became flat and two-dimensional, the anchored boats dark silhouettes tied with bow lines. The girl swam around in the syrupy dimness for a long time.

"How was the water, lovely?" the boathand greeted her when she climbed up the ladder. He told her matter-of-factly the grocery store had been closed.

The man was bent over the ice chest. "Hash for supper tonight," he said with a stiff smile. "Who wants a delicious drink?"

After they ate, while the boathand was washing the dishes below, the man told the girl she shouldn't swim at dusk. "Imagine the explaining I'd have to do," he said, his dark eyes flat in the light of the oil lamp. "Responsible for the untimely death of a bright young actress. Your public would never forgive me."

The girl smiled back at him.

"But really," he said, fatherly, "you could have been run over. These outboards come speeding out of the harbor. They couldn't care less. It's the last thing in the world they're paying attention to."

She felt flattered. "I was staying close to the boats," she said, smiling. Was he scolding her?

He shook his head. "I know these guys. They're maniacs. They don't see you. They run you over. Their propeller chops you up."

"I realized it had gotten dark," she said. "I was being careful."

Charles Howe's face stiffened and his mouth twitched with an odd fury. "You can't be careful if it's someone else who's running you over," he said.

The girl turned to the oil lamp where the flame was stretching with the draft. She put up her palm by the glass opening. The flame bent from side to side, then grew upright and still. There was a clatter of pans down in the hatchway, but the man and the girl ignored it.

He spoke with a lighter, more hollow tone. "I do have to bring you home in one piece." He was asking for her smile. She felt a foreboding but gave him the smile back, aware now that it was long out of her control. He stood up, satisfied, and went below to see what the boathand was up to. Whatever it was, Meg thought, Charles Howe would be disappointed.

The flame near her fluttered again, threatening to go out. Meg watched it and thought of the morning at the motorbike shop. How much she had resented him.

She would not be coming home in one piece after all. She would be run over, chopped up by a propeller, an innocent swimmer in what she knew were dangerous waters. An ingénue.

The Man Who
Would Not Go Away

HE WAS ONE OF those reporters. Never in a place long. Always going away, always coming back. Then he seemed to be around more. Then he was calling me up. I knew he did not have the most promising history with women. I knew that. I kept cool, he kept calling.

Afterward, when things fell apart and he drifted away, well, like fog really, I thought back to those early days when he'd been so persistent. Some men are at their best in pursuit. They put on clean shirts, have a certain gleam in their eye.

Then that gleam fades. He grows distracted, glances off, not wanting to miss the next thing coming along.

Uncertainty is like a drug. It quickens the blood,

wears on the nerves. Slowly it dawned on me this was one of those loose and easy things. Maybe I'll learn something, I thought. I did. I learned things. I learned I didn't have the stomach for it. You need an iron stomach, and nerves of steel.

I was relieved when the man went off, finally, to South Africa. He planned a long stay.

Still, traces of him remained. At first, it was his name. I avoided the people he knew.

But at a dinner party strangers were discussing how the man had been spotted in some exotic locale with a mysterious woman at the end of a very long hall. Where does he find them? one person asked. He keeps them secret, another replied.

Or I end up at a restaurant sitting in the exact same chair I sat in one time with the man. Up his face rises like something out of *The Wizard of Oz,* underlit, ghoulish, laughing in a weird way, really not like the man at all.

I begin to take in more movies than usual. Working for a film magazine I see plenty of movies already. Movies are soothing, they take you out of yourself. But movies can also take you over. Credits begin to drift over me while I'm brushing my teeth or buying a token. A soundtrack swells and I'm in another world. It's not always the best movie. This did not happen when the man was around. When I was with him, I was simply there.

At the club everyone wears black. Metal lawn chairs sit unevenly on the concrete. Women's high heels bob from crossed legs, drinks spill lazily. A long marine tank set into one wall casts off a green glow. The music is deep and relentless and rather stirring. The fish in the tank, oblivious, sealed off, glide slowly in one direction, flip around, glide slowly in the other. Someone taps me on the shoulder.

I move aside and the green light falls on the stranger's face. His eyebrows are raised expectantly. I don't recognize him. Then I do and feel myself blush. I've met him only once. He's a friend of the man's. It acts like an electric conductor, zapping me.

This is not what I expected. This is not what I thought he'd leave behind.

The man's articles appear. In them he's gone on to be another person, one I don't know anymore, off in other worlds. Those worlds begin to matter more.

Everywhere I go people have bad backs, something the man had. In the middle of an interview a director excuses himself to lie down on the editing room floor, just as the man would do, slipping into a back room at a party to lie next to a bed piled with coats. He lay very still, nothing moving but his eyeballs. The only thing to do for a bad back, he'd say, was bear it. It's the sort of thing my father would say.

I swim at the Health Club. A huge tiled room echoing with splashes. Tiny waves teem on the surface, lights make eel reflections. One bullish head plows forward, thunderous kick, frothy wake. At the end of a lane, he tucks into a ball, flips and shoots forward like a torpedo. This time, I don't even dare go in.

I visit my brother who's an investment banker. They've got a house, a baby. My sister-in-law consoles me. "All men are rats," she says and smoothes my brother's forehead adoringly. "Even the angels." The lawn at the back of their house is absolutely unremarkable but in the evenings the space is so tranquil it's mesmerizing with the dark shadows at the edge. The baby crawls on it; to her it's a vast plain. That night when I get into bed I'm exhausted. The leaves are rustling at the window, the man's voice is in them.

Midday, midtown. A man dashing through the bright crowd bears a remarkable resemblance. This was happening a lot. Men across subway platforms. Dark figures sidling in late to movies. A lone soul at the end of a block, rocking on his heels, waiting for a cab. But this fellow, his hair slicked back, was carrying a shopping bag from a lingerie shop, one I knew. Through the curling holes in the bag's design, I could see black lacy things. The man had certain tastes, certain things he liked. His face would become serious and harsh when I tried those things on.

I find pockets of calm. At the museum, past the flower sprays, up the sweeping staircase, I spend

time in the emptier rooms. Flemish paintings, fif-
teenth-century gold frames. There he is, in one,
gripping a sword handle, glancing down in a dis-
dainful way.

Suddenly I have a hundred questions for him,
things I didn't ask before except now that he keeps
appearing I realize how little I knew. Who was he
anyway? Who is he now?

The woman on the hotel staircase was crying. I'd
seen her before in the lobby, smoking, in a strap-
less dress. "I'm *trying* to understand," she said in a
trembling voice to the black-tied fellow at her side.
He held her elbow with a tentative hand as they
moved slowly up the stairs. "You say one thing and
do another," the woman sobbed, too upset to care
if anyone could hear. "There's just so much I can
take." The man mumbled. I couldn't hear what but
a man explaining himself to a woman has a certain
particular tone. The woman cried, "But it's different for a woman!" All hope seemed gone from her
voice.

The library is peaceful. I stack books under the
lampshade, researching articles. Heads at other tables are bent over gently, pages rustle. Shoes clop
by on the wooden floor. The heating vent hums in
the drowsy air. Then I hear his voice behind me. It
says my name.

Going to the movies, people say, is like returning
to the womb. But that's not quite right. Your eyes
are one pair in a galaxy of eyes, all gazing with a

kind of rapture at bright things flickering across a screen. You watch the same movement, have the same current running through your hearts. You're not alone at all.

Things appear at the corner of my eye. A fleeting figure ducking into an alley. Someone fifteen stories up slipping behind a terrace pillar. Across my street curtains close the second I glance over.

I wake in the middle of the night and the man's head is poking through a jagged hole in the wall. His expression is oddly inquisitive, in a scientific way. It is not a look he ever actually gave me.

I once had a conviction having to do with love. I floated on the certainty of it. It had a man's name. But devotion on its own can't last. It is a silly, foolish thing. I thought I knew how to guard against an attachment.

The man and I were driving in the country. He was at the wheel, telling me a story of one of his adventures. He'd been stuck in some wartorn hill town in Central America, barely knowing the language, a deserted place far from everything, not sure if he'd get out alive. He turned his face toward me, talking lazily, making jokes about it. It was evening and growing dark with a moon flickering behind him out the window. He leaned in, looking back and forth between me and the road. We were sealed off, traveling through a darkening world. At one point his eyes meet mine and in that instant

I realized something had come over me and that I was and had been for a while I guess in a new and different state and that it had to do with him. I did not think of it with terror at the time but serenely because the first feeling of love is always serene, and happy. It rejoices. Life has a purpose after all. I kept it to myself, knowing it was not what the man was after, knowing it was in fact what he was running quickly from. But for a while it made me very glad. Then it stopped. And after, it did not go away.